PENGUIN BOOKS

Life on the Farm
The Patti Stories: Volume One

Heather Gardam is a poet and essayist. She lives on Salt Spring Island and is currently sailing the South Pacific with her husband on their schooner. She is at work on Volume Two of *The Patti Stories*.

LIFE ON THE FARM

THE PATTI STORIES: VOLUME ONE

HEATHER GARDAM

Penguin Books

PENGUIN BOOKS

Published by the Penguin Group

Penguin Books Canada Ltd, 10 Alcorn Avenue, Toronto, Ontario, Canada M4V 3B2

Penguin Books Ltd, 27 Wrights Lane, London W8 5TZ, England

Penguin Putnam Inc., 375 Hudson Street, New York, New York 10014, U.S.A.

Penguin Books Australia Ltd, Ringwood, Victoria, Australia

Penguin Books (NZ) Ltd, cnr Rosedale and Airborne Roads, Albany,
Auckland 1310, New Zealand

Penguin Books Ltd, Registered Offices: Harmondsworth, Middlesex, England

First published 2001

1 3 5 7 9 10 8 6 4 2

Manufactured in Canada
Text design and typesetting by Ruthe Swern

Canadian Cataloguing in Publication Data

Gardam, Heather
Life on the farm
(The Patti stories; v. 1)

ISBN 0-14-100420-7
I. Title. II. Series: Gardam, Heather. Patti stories; v. 1.

PS8563.A617L53 2001   jC813'.6   C00-932480-1
PZ.G37Li 2001

Visit Penguin Canada's website at **www.penguin.ca**

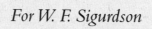

For W. F. Sigurdson

Thanks to Lori Ledingham for her encouragement and help, and to my husband, Bill, who became a great fan of Patti.

Contents

LIFE ON THE FARM

THE PATTI STORIES: VOLUME ONE

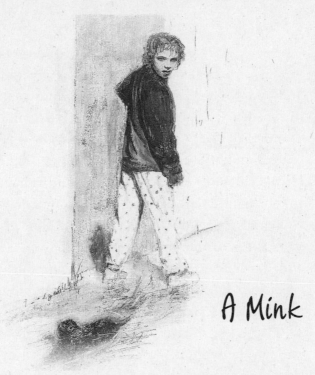

A Mink

PATTI DRIFTED AWAKE. It was still there—the same knot of excitement in her stomach as when she went to bed. That's why the sharp clack of the screen door and her dad's urgent voice from the kitchen didn't alarm her at first—it seemed to fit. It was, after all, her birthday.

"Come quick, Jamie! I need you. Run!"

That sounded strange. The door banged again. Then it opened and Mom called something indistinct out into the dewy June morning. Patti had lifted her head from her pillow to listen, but she still couldn't figure out what was going on.

Something was definitely wrong. Now Patti was up on

her knees, peering out her window. She looked down into the turnaround at the end of the driveway where Mom's little red car was parked and Dad's white pickup, its box still loaded with feed from yesterday. Beyond them, the gate into the barnyard was swinging wide as Jamie disappeared into the wing of the old barn that Dad had rebuilt for the chickens. The door sprang shut behind him.

Patti pulled an old red sweater over her pyjamas. Clutching a pair of dirty socks, she thumped down the stairs and into the kitchen. Half of the big table was set with breakfast things, while the other floury half was taken over by Mom and her enormous clump of bread dough. Mom looked up from kneading.

"Happy birthday, ten-year-old," she said, smiling through the wisps of dark hair that were always escaping from her silver barrette. There was a dusting of flour among the freckles on her nose and cheeks.

"What's happening?" asked Patti.

"There's a mink in the chicken pen," sighed Mom. "The five-week chicks, wouldn't you know." She shook her head in discouragement as her arms continued their rhythmic push and thump. Patti couldn't imagine an event that would disturb this ritual of Saturday bread-making. Sometimes, like today, it bothered her. Didn't Mom want to know what was going on out there? How could she just stay here in the kitchen?

"Would a mink kill them all?" Patti had found her

sneakers in the boot box. She flipped the lid back down and sat on it.

"I don't know yet," Mom shrugged.

"Patti," she said suddenly, stopping for a moment to watch her tie her shoes. "I'm not sure you should go out there right now—not while Dad and Jamie are trying to catch the mink. Why don't you wait till they come back?"

"But I want to see it too!" cried Patti.

"I know, sweetie," said Mom with a little laugh. "But it won't help things if you get in the way."

Patti looked up indignantly.

"I'm ten now, you know," she said, "and it isn't fair!"

"What isn't fair?" Mom asked. Thump, thump went her hands on the dough—the sound was beginning to irritate Patti.

"Jamie gets to milk the cow on weekends and he looks after the chickens when Dad works late at the mill. And . . . and Goldy has been *his* dog since he was ten. He does a whole bunch of things and nobody ever tells him he's in the way."

Patti realized suddenly that she was going to cry in a minute—and when Mom stopped her thumping and looked over at her thoughtfully, well, that made it even worse.

"Anyway, I'll just stand outside the chicken house," Patti said hurriedly, heading for the door. She didn't want to talk any more right now.

But there was nothing happening in the chicken house. It was quiet. She couldn't hear Dad and Jamie talking when she put her ear up to the cracks in the old grey door that looked so odd beside the new cedar planks on this part of the barn.

She scuffed her shoes in the dust for a few moments, kicking a stone in a circle. Then she put her ear to the door again. Had they left already? Where had they gone?

Carefully she lifted the latch and let the door open just a sliver. It was dark inside, except for the warm bright circle cast by the heat lamp—impossible to see into the corners. And it was so quiet. Patti realized suddenly what was missing: the cheeping and pecking sounds of fifty busy chicks had stopped.

She opened the door a crack more.

"No, Patti! No!" Jamie's voice exploded in her ear just as a small black body hurled itself between her legs and slid along the outside of the barn. It had disappeared into a hole in a fraction of a second.

"Oh!" said Patti, looking aghast at Dad and Jamie, who stood, shovels raised. They were lit by a shaft of sunlight through the open door.

"Patti, that was so stupid!" cried Jamie in exasperation. "We almost had him."

Dad and Jamie were standing in different corners of the little room.

"And now he'll just come and get all the *other* chickens."

Jamie's voice was dripping with disgust as he tossed his shovel into the straw.

"Hold on, Jamie," said Dad. "It's not as bad as all that."

But of course it *was*. Patti darted one horrified look around the chicken house—at the piles of limp bodies strewn under the heat lamp, then at Jamie's angry face. She turned and started to run down the lane towards the woods.

"Wait, Patti," she heard Dad call.

Patti had a special tree for times like these. It was a lumpy old apple tree, planted at the end of a row of pear trees, beyond the beehives. She had a stitch in her side by the time she got there; it doubled her over for a few seconds. Then she climbed to the top rail of the zigzag fence and clambered up onto the knotty bottom branch of the tree. In a moment she was hidden behind a veil of bright green, climbing higher towards a patch of blue.

It isn't fair. The thought still throbbed in Patti's chest as she puffed from the run and wiped the tears streaming down her face. She looked through the fresh leaves at the daisy-covered pasture below and all she could think was, "It just isn't fair." They didn't even give her a chance. How was she supposed to know the mink was still there?

But, at the same time, Patti couldn't help remembering Mom's warning. She had been stupid. Jamie was right. And now she was being stupid again, because her tears wouldn't stop. She wanted so badly to be as grown-up as Jamie—to be needed by Dad on the farm. To be a help, not a pest. And look what had happened.

Dad had a song he hummed when he walked. Patti didn't know what it was, except that it was always the same song. "Hmm-*umm*-mm-mm," it went, keeping time with his long strides. She wasn't surprised to hear him coming down the lane to find her. Wiping at the tears impatiently, she began to ease her way down so she could peer at him through the lower branches.

His dark curly hair bulged around his cap, and his blue eyes crinkled up at her.

"We got the mink, Pats," was the first thing he said. "Silly thing didn't want to leave its kill behind—it came slipping in under the wall and even showed us its entrance hole before I killed it with the shovel. Of course, there's probably a family of them. They'll be back if we don't patch all the holes."

"I'm sorry I opened the door, Dad," mumbled Patti.

"I'm sorry that if you had to go opening barn doors today, it had to be *that* one," he answered cheerfully. Then he rubbed his neck.

"Hey," he said, "I'm not supposed to be looking up at you yet. Ten isn't *that* old. When are you coming down? You're giving me a crick."

Patti grinned at him through blurry eyes. But she didn't feel like going home with him just yet.

"Well, when you come back to the house, why don't

you just have a look in the big barn on your way past. Try *that* barn door for a change." He winked at her and headed back between the fruit trees towards the lane.

His hum stopped suddenly as he turned and called to her, "Don't leave it too long, Pats—there's something in the barn that needs to be fed fairly soon."

Needs to be fed?

Patti sat back on the branch of the apple tree to think about that. Could it be . . . ? Excitement began to flutter somewhere in her stomach. No, that's ridiculous, she told herself. She remembered perfectly well the talk with Mom and Dad a few weeks ago about how badly she wanted a pony like her friend Sylvia's. How she had promised she was old enough to look after it all by herself.

"I know you'd do your best, Patti," Mom had answered. "But a pony's a bigger responsibility than you know."

"We just can't afford to buy one, honey," Dad had explained. "There's the saddle and bridle too, you know—and vet bills for worming and so on—and the blacksmith if we put shoes on him."

"But . . . but Sylvia says if you live on a farm like we do, a pony wouldn't hardly cost anything," Patti had argued. "They have to keep *her* pony at a stable and pay for it."

"Well, in a way she's right," Dad had agreed. "But what she doesn't understand is that if you live on a farm like we do, you can't afford to keep an animal that doesn't pay its own way. Don't you see?"

She supposed she did.

"Will we *always* be poor, then?" she had asked.

"Depends what you mean by poor," Mom had answered gently, reaching over to rub a finger on Patti's cheek. "We have a hundred and twenty-five beautiful acres, and we're all healthy and eat well. Sounds rich when you put it that way, don't you think?"

"Some day, Patti," Dad had promised her, then. "Some day you will have your pony."

Some day . . . could that mean today? No, of course not, that wouldn't make sense. It was just a little while ago, when Mom and Dad were asking what she wanted for her birthday. They wouldn't have changed their minds already.

Just the same . . .

Patti slid down to the top of the fence and jumped to the ground.

What *could* it be, then—this something that had to be fed? Not another dog. Not with Goldy so cranky sometimes and set in her ways. Dad had made that clear. And barn cats came and went as they pleased on their farm—sometimes they let you pet them and sometimes they didn't. No, it wouldn't be a cat.

The fact is—and Patti stopped her jogging up the lane to consider this—did she really *want* anything else if she couldn't have a pony? She was walking by now, more slowly all the time. It was her birthday, and Dad had promised a surprise that was waiting in the barn—yet here she was, dragging her feet along the path. She had discovered a new thought and she turned it over and over in her mind: if you wanted something too much, and you knew you couldn't have it, it could spoil a birthday.

I'll try not to want a special thing again, she promised herself . . . or not too much, anyway. She hesitated, then reached cautiously for the latch on the big barn door.

It was dusky inside, but she could see with the first quick look around that there was nothing large and moving in the big entrance bay. It was very quiet.

Something to be fed?

Suddenly, as her eyes became accustomed to the gloom, she saw the bicycle leaning up against one of the centre posts.

She gasped. It was a big bicycle, a *woman*'s bicycle. Was this the surprise? Was it for her? It shone in the shadows, silver, with a blue stripe, every part of it gleaming. Patti stepped closer, her eyes wide with amazement. It had a carry basket and a bell. She reached up tentatively and pulled the lever on the bell. "R . . . aargh!" She gave it a smart pull next time and the "R . . . ing!" filled the barn sweetly. There was a rearview mirror. No one she knew had a rearview mirror on their bicycle. Best of all, from the white rubber handle covers hung blue and white plastic streamers.

A silver bow stuck to the handlebar had a note dangling from it.

"Heigh-ho Silver!" it said. "Love, Mom and Dad."

Silver. That was the Lone Ranger's horse—Dad used to listen to that program on the radio, when he was a boy. What a perfect name for a bike.

Ahh! Suddenly it occurred to her: this was only Dad's joke, that something needed to be fed.

And now there were three laughing faces peering around the barn door.

Patti laughed too. Why, she hadn't even thought of asking for a bike.

"It's *beautiful!*" she exclaimed. She couldn't stop looking at the bicycle.

"I'm afraid it's too big, honey," said Dad apologetically.

"Bigger than mine, that's for sure," said Jamie, as he checked the bell, the mirror, the pump lying neatly along the frame.

"You see, I bought it second-hand from a friend at work who got it for his wife," said Dad. "But she doesn't use it any more. I figured you're growing so fast, and you can manage Jamie's bike okay . . . I'll put blocks on the pedals, so you can reach. Until you grow some more."

"Oh, no, Dad. Please don't." Patti saw the surprise in Dad's face.

"At least not yet," she explained, "till I have a chance to try first. I like it better the way it is."

Mom gave Patti a hug.

"Time to get dressed and have some breakfast," she said.

"Wait a minute! There's something else you haven't noticed," said Dad.

He and Mom exchanged glances. Then he reached into a cardboard box under the bicycle. Out came a small yellow chick, lying still, eyes closed, in the centre of his big calloused hand. It had an angry red spot on the side of its head: Patti's finger pointed this out.

"Yep," he said, "the mink bit this one too, but not hard enough to kill. I think it might live, with some care. But the big hens would go after it if I put it in with them. And it seems such a pity to put it down now, after surviving that dratted mink. Will you look after it till it can take care of itself?"

He shook his head ruefully. "I'm afraid this is more like a job I've given you here. Not a real birthday present."

Patti reached for the chick and tucked its limp warmth against her sweater.

"What do I feed it?" she asked.

"I have a bag of chick grain," Dad said. "But I think you'll need an eyedropper filled with warm water to dribble over its beak every hour or so for a while—till it's up and pecking."

"Sort of like a miniature milk bottle," said Jamie.

"Breakfast," said Mom more firmly this time. "Come on, everybody."

"In a few minutes, okay?" Patti was thinking hard.

"First, I'd better find the eyedropper and do the

warm-water thing. It's sort of an emergency, don't you think? A good spot for it would be the summer kitchen, warm and away from the cats . . ."

"And I'll need a bigger cardboard box than that one, too," she decided. "Do you think we can find one?"

Dad considered for a moment.

"Yep," he said at last, as his eyes crinkled with a smile. "It sounds like we're in business, doesn't it?"

Two Bricks
Short of a Load

PATTI WAS STILL STRUGGLING WITH THE FRAYED KNOT
in her laces when she heard the screen door bang.

"Wait," she yelled. "Wait for me!"

She gave the knot one last yank so that it came away in
her hand.

"Darn, darn darn." She stuffed the whole mess in her
pocket and flip-flopped in her gaping shoe to the door.

"No, Patti." Her mother was clanking breakfast dishes
into the sink. "You'll have to find something to tie that
shoe with if you're going out to the hayfield today."

"But he's gone, Mom. Jamie's gone already."

"Here." Mom had found a roll of orange hay-baling

twine in the junk drawer. She considered Patti's undone shoe, then grabbed the kitchen scissors and cut a piece of twine.

"It'll do for now," she said. "I'm late for work. But you'll have to let me tie it—it's slippery. It won't stay done up unless it's really tight."

Patti brushed the stubborn wisps of hair from her eyes and glared at the top of her mother's bent head, her lips a straight, angry line. She was ten years old and her mom was tying her shoelaces. It had to be *perfect*, of course. Jamie was way ahead of her now, but Mom still had to do things *perfectly*.

Mom gave her foot a friendly little smack and stood up. When she saw Patti's face, she suddenly pulled her into a tight hug.

"Cheer up, Patti baby," she laughed. "You've got the whole day and the whole summer holidays to catch up."

Patti's hand was impatient on the doorknob, but Mom was still talking.

"Just one more second, okay? I can't make it home from town for lunch—Dad is getting away from the mill at noon, so we can go to the bank and sign for the new loan. But you be sure you and Jamie come back and get some food. Promise? I'll phone you from the bank."

Patti nodded and was gone.

The lane was pocked with dried-out mudholes and cow flops. Patti had a special way to get around them all, even when she was in a hurry. She pretended she was on a horse. She stood in front of the first hollow for a moment to get her breath, then she began her routine: one two three four, one two three four. The important thing was to take exactly four steps before she jumped each danger spot, and not to change the beat—which meant some quick think-ing when the gaps were big. Patti was getting good at it. She sang something new as she trotted: "Two—bricks—short—of a load. Two—bricks—short—of a load."

What did it mean? It was something about Maynard, she guessed. Dad had muttered it under his breath last night at suppertime. But when she asked him to explain, he had remembered suddenly that it was her bath time. Grown-ups shouldn't *say* things if they don't want to explain them, she decided. She landed with a firm two-foot smack at the end of the lane.

Jamie was nowhere in sight as she crossed the stream, but she could hear the baler grinding and sputtering. Dad must be happy, anyway, that Maynard managed to get the old tractor going again. He had worked on it all yesterday afternoon until late, pushing back his baseball cap often to scratch his thinning hair and look at the var-ious parts spread out on the grass. Jamie handed him the tools he needed, while Patti watched, hands in her pock-ets. Maynard had promised that Jamie could drive the tractor today.

"Me too?" Patti had asked. Jamie laughed scornfully, but

Maynard's eyes twinkled at her as from under the peak of his cap.

"When you're twelve, like Jamie, little sprat, and your feet can reach the pedals."

Later, at supper, Jamie had proudly explained to Mom and Dad about fixing the tractor—how *he* had been the one to solve the problem in the end by suggesting that they check the battery. When he heard that, Dad suddenly thumped the table with his fist.

"That should have been the *first* thing he checked. I should be here on the farm." His face was red with anger.

"I hate spending all my time at that dratted mill. The whole farm depending on a hired hand."

Dad was often angry about the mill.

That was when he said that funny thing that had been singing in Patti's head ever since: "Two bricks short of a load."

Patti was puffing as she came at last to the three beehives at the corner of the wood lot. She flopped on the grass in the early sun to watch the bees go in and out. There were dozens of them coming back from the field already, their back legs so round with pollen that they were having trouble landing. She looked carefully to see if she could spot a worker doing a "bee dance" to tell the others where the best nectar was. Well, it was probably too late in the morning for that. They were hard at work now—far too busy for dances. They were too busy even to notice her.

She wriggled up so close to the entrance board that she could feel the breeze in her hair when the next bees came in for a landing. She hugged her elbows and lay absolutely still, smothering a little giggle.

She knew more about bees, she guessed, than most people her age. Definitely more than Jamie, who was two years older. Maybe some day she could do all the bee work for Dad. Mr. Wallace was nice, but he was so old and slow. She came down the lane to watch him whenever he worked the bees. He mumbled all the time through his bushy moustache and his big, square face-net which was tied tightly over a battered straw hat, then crossed around the thin chest of his stooping white coveralls to keep the bees away from his face.

He mumbled to his bees mostly. But when his smoker was working well at keeping the bees quiet, he would let Patti come in really close to look at the frames. He was teaching her to tell the difference between the honey cells and the brood cells. And the larvae that would turn into drones or queens. But he would never let her into the shed to help with extracting the honey.

"No siree, little one—you can't depend on bees while you're busy taking their house apart. You'll just have to wait till you're big enough to fit my extra coveralls and net."

Patti sighed as she gave the hives one last look and headed towards the woods. That would be *years*.

The bush-lot was dark after the sunshine of the meadow, but that didn't bother her any more—not since she was six. Besides, the path, wide and well-beaten from cows and tractors, headed straight for the bright field beyond the trees.

As she blinked for a moment at the edge of the wood where the sun was bright on the crisp, golden stubble, she suddenly realized that the tractor noises had stopped. Maynard and Jamie—what were they doing? They were wandering around among the new bales, kicking at them here and there in the strangest way. Then they came together to kick at the same bale.

"What's going on?" she called, zigzagging at a trot among the tight hay packages. She peered around Jamie just in time to see Maynard kick one last time at a sad little heap of hay and tangled twine, then flick his lighter and set it on fire.

"How come?" she cried.

"Baler's not working right," said Jamie. "This one's too big a mess to do anything with."

"That's right," said Maynard. "The others ain't so bad—we'll mark 'em and load 'em separate. Not too many, anyways. Gotta get the baler fixed, though." He chewed anxiously on a dry piece of hay.

"I dunno. Your dad's always done that kinda thing before." He stooped beside her to watch the quick blaze. Patti was surprised to smell beer on his breath so early in the morning.

The fire crackled hot and high and smokeless for a few moments. They watched, the heat smarting their cheeks. Each separate stalk of hay glowed brightly before it fell apart in a puff of ashes and disappeared. As it reached the bottom of the pile, the line of flame wriggled like a snake, then moved out swiftly into the surrounding stubble.

"Damn!" said Maynard. He ran to the tractor nearby. He tossed a rake at Jamie, grabbed the shovel himself and ran back to beat at the little circle moving relentlessly outwards. Patti watched for a little while, then she dabbed cautiously at the hot line with her foot.

"No, Patti!" yelled Maynard. "Look, you take this. I'm gettin' some water and sacks from the barn." He dropped the shovel and ran to unhook the tractor from the baler. Patti and Jamie heard him roar into the woods as they began to beat at the edges of the steadily growing patch of scorched grass.

"Let's put it out before he gets back," said Jamie. His face was flushed from the fire and his eyes were excited as he lifted the rake high in the air, flinging up little puffs of smoke each time he thumped the ground.

"Yah!" Patti tried to sound enthusiastic too, but the shovel was a big one with a very long handle. Jamie hit at the fire again and again with the rake, but she could barely manage to lift the shovel at all or smack it down in the right place. She tried dragging the metal part over the fire, but that didn't work either. The flame jumped up brighter than ever as soon as she moved on.

"No, stupid!" shouted Jamie. "You're wasting time. Here, let me take the shovel. It might be faster than the rake."

They were relieved to hear the tractor again, a few minutes before it erupted from the woods. Maynard had attached the small tool trailer behind it. Patti watched as it jagged wildly back and forth among the hay bales, while the water in the big buckets slopped and splashed.

Maynard showed them how to dump the potato sacks into the water, then hit at the fire with them. In a very short time it was all over. Only a few wisps of smoke and steam still drifted into the air.

"Well," said Maynard, as he pushed his cap back with one hand and scratched his head with his thumb, "I've made a big enough mess for one mornin'. Guess I'll head off to lunch early today.

"Say, if you kids want to mark the bad bales with some of that there coloured tape on the tractor, we'll pick 'em up on the trailer when I get back."

They watched him trudge across the field, kicking here and there at rocks. His hands were jammed into the back pockets of his jeans so that his elbows waved disjointedly as he walked. He ducked through the fence, then took the path around the neighbour's uncut wheat towards the road. It was the shortcut to town.

"Poor Maynard," said Patti. "Maybe lunch will make him feel better."

"Lunch. Hah!" Jamie sounded like Dad sometimes. "I bet it's the bar. I bet it's beer, not lunch."

"Maybe he's having lunch at the bar," insisted Patti, her chin in the air.

"Don't be stupid," said Jamie. "Let's get to work. We'll get it all done before he comes back."

"Yah!" Patti ran to get the roll of fluorescent pink tape and some shears from the tool box on the tractor. Jamie kicked the partly ruined bales while Patti cut pieces of tape and handed them to him. Then Jamie tied them on to the loose part of the twine. They were getting the job done fast.

"They look like presents," said Patti. "One, two, three, four . . . oh, look, Jamie!"

The fire was suddenly alive again. But it was no small wriggling snake this time. It had reached another bale already, and now it was raging. Somehow they hadn't noticed the breeze getting up. They could see, along the far side of the black patch, a short wall of flame bending before the wind and rushing outwards.

"Quick!" cried Jamie. "We have to stop it before it reaches any more bales."

They grabbed a potato sack each, dropped it in the water, then dashed towards the leading curve of fire.

Whap, whap went the sacks on the ground. But it wasn't so easy this time. It was different. Each time they doused a small part of the line, the section of fire beside it leaped sideways to fill in the gap. The wind gusted stronger.

"It's no good," yelled Jamie. "It's too fast for us. I'll have to run next door and call the fire department."

He ran to the fence and ducked through. He turned on the other side and, cupping his hands to his mouth, he shouted, "Patti! Just keep it out of Mr. Hardy's wheatfield!"

Patti could hardly hear him over the wind and the snapping of the fire. She dipped her sack into the bucket on the trailer, then she jumped down and ran to an arm of flame that was reaching towards the neighbour's field. Whap, whap, whap, whap. Got it, she thought. Got that one. She skipped back to the trailer, soaked the bag again, then ran to the next jag of fire poking out. One, two, three, four. Got that one too, she thought with satisfaction. I'm doing it. I'm going to get this all out before Jamie comes back. The trouble was, she was starting to feel a bit tired already. Too bad Maynard hadn't put the buckets on the ground. Too bad the trailer was so far away from the fire now.

Run to the trailer. Climb up. Dip the bag. Pull it out, dripping water all over your shoes. Jump down. Run to that angry, darting flame.

"Two—bricks—short—of a load," puffed Patti.

There, that one's out. Run back to the trailer, again and again. But she was losing her breath, she was hot, and the stitch in her side was getting worse.

Suddenly two sounds at once broke into her world of wind and wild crackling: a fire truck clanged out of the woods at the same moment that the fire, with a great swoosh and roar, pounced hungrily at last on Mr. Hardy's standing wheat.

"Oh no." Patti stood, her breath hurting her chest, wet bag hanging limply at her side. She watched the fire. It was too much for her now. There was nothing more that she could do.

Patti lay full length in the warm bath water while Mom scrubbed gently at the hardest patches of soot on her legs. Ten years old, she thought sleepily, and Mom is giving me a bath. But somehow it didn't seem to matter.

"That was the fire chief on the phone just now," Mom was telling her. "He wanted to know if your proper name is Patricia, so he can put it in his report to the newspaper. He says it's because of you and Jamie that they saved Mr. Hardy's wheatfield."

Patti was feeling fine now. But suddenly she remembered that dreadful moment earlier when she hadn't felt good at all.

"It's horrible, Mom, when a fire gets away from you, even though you've done your best. Even when you've tried your hardest to do everything all by yourself."

Mom stopped scrubbing to look at Patti.

"You know what?" said Patti.

Mom shook her head and waited.

"I saw Maynard feeling that way too. Even before the big fire started."

"Did you?"

There was something still bothering Patti.

"Mom, why did Dad say that thing about Maynard—'two bricks short of a load'? Does it mean he isn't smart enough?"

"Oh, Patti." Mom shook her head wearily. Her grin looked a little twisted.

"It's hard to explain. Maynard is special just the way he is. It was an unkind thing for Dad to say. A thoughtless thing. But I think Dad was really talking about himself as much as anyone."

"How come?"

"I think he was trying to say that there are always *too many* bricks on a load these days. For Dad, because he has to work at the mill *and* run the farm. For me, because I have to work at the bank, even though there's so much to do here at home. And Maynard especially—he was hired to *help* Dad, not do most of the work by himself. You kids, too. We expect a lot of you."

"So, you mean, no one can be smart enough if there's just too much to do?" asked Patti.

Mom's eyes were a little wet and she wiped at them briefly with a hand that was even wetter. She didn't answer.

"Now we're lots of *burned bales* short of a load," Patti announced drowsily.

Mom suddenly snorted with laughter. She was quiet for a moment, kneeling beside the tub, chin cupped in her hands.

"I guess what I'm trying to say," she said at last, "is that grown-ups can do and say some pretty thoughtless things when they get pushed too hard . . ." She stood up then, and grabbed a towel to hold out for Patti. "Good thing they have kids around to pull their chestnuts out of the fire, eh, Pats?"

Pull their chestnuts out of the fire? Patti's eyes were beginning to close. She would think about *that* one tomorrow.

Threshing

PATTI'S BIKE LEANED AGAINST THE PLUM TREE beside the summer kitchen door. It was clean and polished, its basket filled: ironed white sheets for tablecloths, Mom's best salt and pepper shakers, some empty pint jars and a handful of cosmos and daisies, fresh from the garden. Patti would be leaving soon to pedal the two and a half miles to the McLean farm. That's where the threshers would go for lunch today.

This year was different—she would be a server, not just one of the little kids who had to stay out of the way on the back lawn until someone called them in to eat. The trouble was, she wasn't quite sure what a server was supposed to do.

"Don't worry," Mom had reassured her. "Mrs. McLean will tell you exactly what she wants you to help with."

Luckily, her friend Ruth would be there too.

Mom's kitchen smelled of apple pies. Patti, coming back from the chicken pen, where she had dumped the apple peelings, was met with the warm scent of baking through the screen door.

She settled once more on the stool beside the apple peeler: one more bowl of apples to go. It was a nice job. She loved the long curly strip of peel, the continuous loop of apple slices—that is, if she was careful how she fastened on the apple to start with. You take your time with that, clamping the apple carefully through its north pole and south pole, then with a "whirr" on the handle it was done, like magic.

Mom had rolled out all the pastry by now, and draped the crust in the bottom of the waiting pie plates. In all—including the ones cooling on racks, the ones in the oven, a row of five ready to be baked and two more waiting for Patti's apple slices—there were fifteen pies. Fifteen apple pies.

"Shouldn't you be on your way by now?" Mom asked.

There was a strange flutter in the pit of Patti's stomach. It had seemed such an exciting idea, going to the McLeans' farm by herself to help set up the tables, while Mom finished the pies and brought them in the car later. But in the last few minutes she had begun to wonder: did she even know how to find the McLeans' back door?

What if she did something wrong? It wouldn't be the same as going with Mom or Dad.

Mom liked Mrs. McLean a lot. But Patti found her abrupt, as if she expected kids to just automatically *know* the rules of her house. Like taking off your shoes at the door, for instance. Luckily Patti had already been told about that. It was something Patti had noticed before: how grown-ups were often different when they talked to kids by themselves, without their parents. Would Mrs. McLean be like that?

Mom had stopped stirring apples and sugar and cinnamon in the big white bowl and was watching Patti peel an apple very, very slowly. She already knew how fast she could do it—now she wanted to see how slowly the handle could turn and still peel and slice properly.

"It's less than an hour till I have to be there too," Mom said. "Run along now, honey. That's enough apples—and Ruth will be looking for you."

All summer Patti had ridden her bike along the road between the Smiths' farm to the east and the Rogers' to the west. She had discovered how different things looked from a big bike—different from walking or driving in a car. Perched high up on the seat, she would push hard on the pedal that was up, then wait, reaching down with the other toe until the next pedal came around. She didn't need blocks, as Dad thought she might. It wasn't fast, but it was okay. And because it was such a big bike—bigger than Jamie's—she could see above the alders and weeds that crowded the ditches.

She could see the fields, some of them already cut and stooked, waiting for the threshing crew. They stretched down to the creek and forest to the right, and down to another creek and a smaller wood on the left. Cloud shadows raced across them as her tires hummed along the pavement.

Best of all, from this height she could check every day on two bay horses where they grazed two fields below the road. Lately she was beginning to suspect that they watched for her too, always lifting their heads as she wheeled her wide turn at the neighbour's driveway. How could they hear her, anyway, from so far away?

Today, with chaff in the breeze on her face, and the noise of the thresher in the distance, she waved gaily at the horses with their pricked ears and continued right around the bend, the road stretching on and on into new biking territory. But there was no more time for Patti to savour the strangeness of the road—she could already see the crowd of parked cars along the McLeans' driveway, and was busy looking for spaces between them to wobble through. Then she was pushing her bike towards the laughter and chatter of the open back door.

"Ah, here she is!" said Mrs. McLean while Patti was still lifting a tentative hand to tap on the door frame. "Leave your shoes on today, dear!"

And the next thing she knew, she was part of a team of women and children that carried chairs, arranged flowers, took trays of lemonade to the kids out back. There were great bursts of laughter from a kitchen that smelled of roast chicken and stuffing. It was so crowded with extra tables for holding the casseroles and salad bowls from each new person that arrived, there was hardly even room to move. Patti rarely knew what the jokes were about, but she laughed too, and so did Ruth, as they raced each other through the table setting.

Then, if she thought the house was noisy before, it fairly rocked when the men and teenagers began to arrive. They were red-faced and soaked with sweat, but the jokes and laughter never faltered as they stood in clumps and lines for the kitchen pump and the downstairs bathroom.

There were eighteen places at the long table that had been extended from the dining room into the living room. Patti knew they would eat in shifts—first the men and older boys and girls who pitchforked the stooks onto wagons and fed the thresher, then the younger ones, like Jamie, who carried the water buckets and drove tractors. Next it would be time to bring in the little ones from the backyard. Only then would it be the turn of the kitchen team.

Would there be any food left? Patti's question was met with yet another great boom of laughter from everyone within hearing distance as they turned to look again at the food stacked on the kitchen tables.

Of course, each round of eaters meant another set of dishes to be washed, dried and replaced along the table.

"You'll earn your dinner today, Patti," Mrs. McLean announced gaily just as Mom arrived, flushed and breathless, and asking for some carriers to help her with the pies.

But by now Patti had decided that serving was fun. She and Ruth had been given the dining-room end of the long table. Back and forth to the kitchen they bustled, with a fresh basket of buns, a dish of pickles or onion sauce or crabapple jelly to be refilled. They whispered and giggled whenever they collided in the hall.

Dad was in her section, and so was Maynard.

"Excuse me, Miss," Dad said nearly every time she passed, her borrowed apron swishing against her shorts as she rushed here and there, "but couldn't you move a bit faster?" She grinned at him or punched him on the shoulder if she had a hand free.

Maynard winked at her occasionally when she caught his eye, and once he asked her politely for a fresh pitcher of water. But even in this crowd of people, she felt uncomfortable with Maynard. A distance had been growing between them ever since the grass fire, although that was weeks ago. It was as if he suddenly didn't know how to tease any more. As if Patti had forgotten how to talk to him. She never helped him in his work around the farm these days. She would rather ride her bike.

Yet he was still her friend, she was sure of that. Dad

hadn't acted impatiently with him since the fire, which was a bit of a puzzle to her. Yet it made her happy too. Once, when Jamie made a joke about setting the hay bales on fire, Dad told him sharply to mind his tongue. Still . . . Patti shrugged as she headed for the kitchen with an empty pitcher. She always ended up shrugging when she tried to figure out this thing about Maynard.

Old Mr. Keldon was sitting beside Dad.

"Whose little girl are you?" he had asked with a twinkle in his blue eyes when she first brought their plates. Later, she had fetched him the bowl of stuffing that had wandered somehow to another section of the table. He looked so small and wrinkled—a little gnome among a thicket of elbows—and his colour was grey next to the burly redness of her father. He was quiet, too, in the midst of the clanking of dishes and the joking back and forth. Then Patti looked across the table and was stunned to see that his head was down, that it rested right on his plate. His shoulders were limp.

Hand to her mouth, Patti watched as the shock registered first on the person opposite him, then the one next to him, then finally her father. Silence grew around Mr. Keldon, but still nobody moved.

Suddenly Maynard was on his knees beside him, calling gently, "Jim? Jim?"

He looked up to say urgently to Mrs. McLean, "Jen, phone for the ambulance. Quick!"

In a moment he had gathered the old man like a child in his arms and was making his way behind the crowded chairs, lifting his burden high to squeeze through the gaps.

"I'll get a blanket for the couch," said one of the women, as if she had just woken up.

"No, bring it to my pickup," said Maynard. "I'll head right on out to meet the ambulance. We better not wait."

The screen door banged behind him. His engine roaring into action was the signal for talking to begin again around the tables. It was quiet talk, though. The workers attacked their dinners now as if they had just remembered that their main purpose was to finish and get back to the fields as soon as possible. It was as if Mrs. McLean's blanket had been dropped over them all, Patti thought. Even Jamie and his friends ate quickly and quietly, making way for the younger children.

But Patti's feet were beginning to drag long before all the children had finished their pie and ice cream. She was glad to be given a tea towel and a stool to prop herself on as she dried the forks and spoons that had been dropped into a bucket of rinse water beside her. She listened to the buzz of conversation around her.

". . . his heart?"

"Seems to me his older brother—you know Richard? Down by the lumber yard? Didn't he have a stroke?"

"Yes, that's right. This was probably a stroke too, come to think of it. Poor Jim."

Stroke. Patti thought about that word. It made her think of lightning, of a sword that could cut through all the talking and eating here in the house. The pitching and shouting and tractor noises going on and on out in the sunny fields. It could strike way back to the time of ploughing and planting in the spring, then the cutting and stooking, anxiously watching the weather. And the days and days of cooking in all the farm kitchens. A stroke could make everything pointless. It could make even the grown-ups feel helpless.

But not Maynard. Patti stopped drying a bundle of forks as that idea caught her by surprise. Maynard had not been helpless at all, had he? She remembered how quickly he had moved to help Mr. Keldon, how easily he had lifted and carried him away. If a stroke hit her, she decided, it would certainly be a lucky thing to have Maynard around.

The road back from the McLeans' farm didn't look so different, after all, from her usual bit of road, thought Patti. It really wasn't very far from home: she could look across to her own fields before she even reached the bend. She was pedalling standing up because she was tired now, and somehow that seemed to take less effort than sitting on the seat, stretching and reaching for the pedals.

It was only three-thirty, but Mom had sent her home to feed the chickens and check on the dog and take a casserole out of the freezer. Dad and Jamie would go to another farm for dinner tonight. They wouldn't get home till after dark. Mom still had another hour of cleaning up to do, she said, before she could leave the McLeans'.

Patti got off her bike to look at the horses, who, as usual, had stopped their grazing to watch her.

A truck cruised up towards her and pulled over into the gravel.

"Givin' that silver horse of yours a rest, sprat?"

It was Maynard, his head sticking out of the window, with half a cigarette balanced on his lower lip.

Patti pointed over the fields to the real horses to explain why she had stopped. She still couldn't think of anything to say.

Maynard gave a little goodbye wave and revved his engine.

"No, wait!" called Patti suddenly. "How is Mr. Keldon? Was it a stroke?"

Maynard looked surprised. He pushed his cap back and scratched the top of his head.

"He'll be okay," he said, in a moment. "It'll take a while, but they think he'll be all right."

"Are you going back to the fields now?"

"Yep," he said. "Reckon we got a bit more to do yet."

Patti suddenly wished Mom hadn't given her a job to do at home. It would be fun to go and watch the threshing from Maynard's truck.

"Do you think I could drive the tractor next summer?" she asked. Maynard looked at her consideringly.

"Seems like your legs are stretchin' out pretty good," he said at last. "That bike sure helps." He laughed. "But you're gonna need at least another couple years of growin', seems to me. And some practice," he added, with a wink.

"Will you teach me?" Patti asked.

"Next summer we'll get you started for sure," Maynard promised.

He waved again and pulled away with a little scrunch of gravel.

"See ya," Patti called after him happily, as she wheeled her bike back on to the road.

Chicky (Part 1)

"SAY GOOD NIGHT, CHICKY," SAID PATTI.

She stood in the doorway and reached her hand into the living room where Mom and Dad were reading. Jamie was sitting on the floor in front of the radio. The wood stove crackled for the first time that fall.

"Go on," urged Patti, "say good night!"

On her wrist perched a small, reddish brown, smoothly fledged young chicken. It poked its head up and down, up and down, for a good look into the brightly lit room.

"Say good night," said Patti again.

"Barr-gh!" announced the chicken, just as it had every night for the past week.

Mom and Dad and Jamie burst into laughter. They just couldn't get used to it. In Patti's family, chickens weren't given special treatment. They were outdoor creatures, to be watered and fed every day, their house mucked out every week or two. Patti and Mom, who collected the eggs from the laying chickens, treated *them* to kitchen scraps and sometimes even gave them names like Mrs. Cross or Smoothy if they were either especially pecky or sweet-tempered enough to allow their silky feathers to be stroked. But all the rest of the chickens came and went unremarked—raised only for production, like most other things on a farm.

And now here was Chicky, the sole survivor of a mink attack. She had been hand-fed by Patti since she was five weeks old, so she knew nothing about the regular life of chickens. What she knew mostly was Patti. Every morning she was lifted gently from the cardboard box beside the stove in the summer kitchen and popped outside on the back steps. Her dish was heaped with chicken pellets, her water container cleaned and filled. All day she patrolled the strip of grass that edged the old farmhouse—back and forth, up and down, she scratched for bugs and worms. As she grew bigger, she had even begun to follow Patti whenever she heard the tell-tale thump of running shoes on the steps and the bang of the screen door.

"Look, Mom," Patti had called the first time, as she led the little chicken in a figure-eight around the yard.

Then it became a nuisance. Twice she had to stop and pop Chicky into her bicycle basket and bring her back down the long driveway from the road. These last few days, Patti had started to sneak quietly out of the house, dodge around the trees, then crouch down by the fence to see if she had escaped from Chicky. It didn't seem funny any more.

Lately, as September chilled and it began to get dark while they were still eating supper, Chicky would jump up on one of the outside window sills to peck "rat-a-tat-tat," at the glass, reminding Patti that it was time for chickens to be safely tucked away from owls.

And that was how the good-night ritual had started.

"She looks like a falcon, sitting on your wrist like that," chuckled Dad over his reading glasses. Patti had just come back from putting Chicky away in her box.

"You two should be in the circus."

"Or the Fall Fair," said Jamie idly. Then he suddenly sat up.

"Hey!" he exclaimed. "That's a good idea. You could go in the pet category."

"A chicken?" Patti's first thought was to laugh. Yet, why not?

The pet class in the Fall Fair was fun to watch. Every-thing from terrified barn cats to turtles were paraded by loving owners, in their arms and on leashes—even, in the case of a boa constrictor one year, in a red wagon—around the fenced enclosure. Sometimes both child and pet would be dressed in a costume, often a long dress for a little girl and a baby bonnet for her kitten. The crowd clapped and ahh'd and hooted with laughter. Then came the opportunity for the children and their pets to do a demonstration, if they wanted to. That was the exciting part, because sometimes they performed the most astonishing routines together. And that's what interested Patti most—co-operation between animals and humans.

Goldy, their old golden Labrador, had taken her turn in the pet class two years ago. But, to Jamie's embarrassment and the rowdy delight of the spectators, when Goldy's chance came to roll over and jump a hurdle, she had simply ignored Jamie's pleading and all his patient training. Instead, she sat and gazed with dignified disdain into the distance. Nothing could change her opinion. She won a prize, though—a blue rosette with "Forget It! Award" written in black pen in the centre. Jamie came around eventually to see the joke. He still had the rosette pinned to his bedroom wall, among all his hockey and basketball certificates.

But when it came to entering a Fall Fair class, Patti knew what she *really* wanted: a pony. She wanted to be part of the special events that took place in the riding ring at the outer edge of the grounds. There, dodging among the crowd, straining for a good view, Patti listened to the far-off hum and chatter and jokes over the loudspeaker, the shrieks of children and announcements of winners and events, and it all seemed to belong to a frivolous, holiday world.

This was more serious stuff. Here at the riding ring, nobody ever laughed or called out when a youngster, dressed in a formal jacket and hard hat, face stiff with concentration, walked his pony around the fence, then trotted, cantered and left the ring to a polite smatter of applause. And later, when the jumps came out, and a horse and rider managed to slip over the final gate without sending anything clattering to the ground, there was always a sigh, a general release of breath. As if everyone there had been involved in the success.

The horse show was where Patti had spent most of her Fall Fair days for the past two years. Early in the morning she would help Dad and Maynard unload their Jersey cow Buttercup, who always won a ribbon in the milking class. Then, she made a quick check of the baking section, to see how her decorated cake had done, and the preserves section to see how Mom's pickles had fared. Finally, she would hurry to the part of the building that displayed children's projects. There, she met Ruth and her school friends to admire each other's model airplanes, carved vegetables, log houses and knitted doll clothes, which covered the walls and shelves.

Then they all trooped off together to the centre ring. Mid-morning was the time for the pet show, and nobody wanted to miss that.

Afterwards, grabbing her lunch bag from the pickup, Patti would disappear to watch the horses for the rest of the day. This year her friend Sylvia would be entering her pony in the show. Maybe she could help her—hold the reins, perhaps. How Patti envied her.

But what about Jamie's idea of putting Chicky in the Fall Fair? Patti had her book open as she lay on her stomach on the carpet, but she was thinking, not reading.

It wasn't anything *like* having your own pony in the horse show . . . Patti looked quickly up at Mom and Dad the moment she thought this. She didn't want them to realize how badly she still wanted a pony—it seemed unfair to them, somehow. She knew they would give her one if they could. So, ever since her birthday, she had been careful not to mention the topic. But the dream was never far away.

"Maybe I *will* put Chicky in the Fair," Patti announced suddenly to her startled family in the warm living room.

"What's a falcon?" Patti asked Mr. Wallace the next day. Seeing his small van in the yard when she came home from school, she had skipped quickly down the lane to the shed beside the beehives in the bottom pasture. The old bee-keeper was tidying away tools and frames for the winter.

"It's a hawk—a bird of prey," said Mr. Wallace. "In the old days, the rich people—the lords of the manors—would capture these wild birds, then have them trained for hunting."

"Hunting what?" asked Patti

"Rabbits, small birds, whatever was the natural prey of the falcon," he answered. "They would bring down their kill for their masters."

"How could you train a hawk to do that?" asked Patti.

"Well, I suppose it's a lot like keeping bees."

Mr. Wallace had stopped work and squatted on the steps of the shed. His eyes, a grey-blue under surprising black brows, shone whenever he had a chance to explain bees to Patti.

"Whenever you think a person has trained some wild creature," he said, "always look carefully at what is really happening. You'll see that what is going on is mostly co-operation. It might *look* like training. But it's not."

Patti was puzzled.

"Never forget this," he said. "My bees would collect honey, raise their brood and replace their queens whether they were in hives or out in the forest in some hollow tree somewhere. All I do is watch them carefully and learn what their instinctive behaviour is. Then I take that knowledge and use it. I provide the wax frames and strong boxes for them to live in so they don't have to build. They can spend their extra time collecting honey for me. But if I make a mistake—take away too much honey or mis-manage the brood—then poof! They're gone. Off in a swarm to find a tree somewhere."

"Training?" Mr. Wallace nudged Patti's arm, his eyes crinkling with laughter. "Don't let anyone fool you," he said. "It's the *humans* who end up getting trained, whether it's bees or falcons."

"What about horses?" asked Patti.

"Horses too," said Mr. Wallace.

Dusk had crept up on them as they talked.

"I'm going to have to come back again tomorrow," he said. "I've gone and talked my time away."

"I'll come straight down after school and help you," Patti promised.

And she was glad she did, because Mr. Wallace had brought a surprise for her, wrapped in a plastic bag.

"It's a library book," he said, "so I'll have to get it back from you in a couple of weeks."

It was a big book with beautifully detailed illustrations of castles and medieval farms and ordinary people, busy in their daily activities. She sat for a long time that evening, studying the drawings of herb gardens and strange, thatched, dome-shaped beehives. The pictures gave a view from above, a bird's-eye view.

She turned to the section on falconry. A fierceness to these pictures surprised Patti. There were heavy leather gloves on the men, and hoods, leather bands and long leashes on the big birds. Jesses, the leather bands were called. But there was a proud beauty too, of horses and men and wild hunting birds grouped on a hilltop against a blue summer sky. They were all intent on the same prey, the same outcome. Patti looked carefully at the illustrations. The women, clustered to one side, rode sidesaddle and carried smaller hawks. All the costumes were richly coloured, and the horses were almost as ornately decorated as the people.

These were the aristocrats, the people with money and leisure to spend on such entertainment. They were as different from the simple farm folk she had looked at on the previous pages as the falcons were different from the chickens that scratched in the doorways of the peasants.

There had always been a few people in the world who got to do the exciting things, she reflected. They were born luckier than others. So . . . even in the old days there were people to envy, the way she envied Sylvia with her pony. Yet her friend Sylvia was so nice. Patti liked her a lot. When you came right down to it, people were just people. And birds were just birds.

Suddenly Patti laughed. Of course! *Birds* were just *birds*.

Chicky (Part II)

"GETTING SOME IDEAS FOR THE FALL FAIR?" asked Dad, as he looked up from his paper several days later. He was pleased that Patti had taken him up on his idea of falcons. But he was puzzled, too. Riding on Patti's wrist was one thing—it was cute, no doubt about it. But there was a big difference between a young chicken and a falcon. What could Chicky actually *do*?

"I've had a wonderful idea," said Patti smugly. "But don't bother asking. Just don't bother."

"Come on," teased Dad. "You can't keep a secret for two whole weeks."

Dad was right—it *was* hard to keep it a secret. It seemed

that no matter where she took Chicky to practise, behind the house or in the big barn, either Jamie or Maynard would suddenly appear. And it was especially difficult to ask Mom's help with the sewing machine or to find scraps of leather and some grey woolly material. How could she explain what they were for? Luckily, Mom hadn't asked any questions yet.

Working with Chicky was the easiest part of all. The little chicken always waited close to the back steps, eager to follow Patti wherever she led. Since her feed dish was only partly filled in the mornings now, and the rest of her food seemed to ride around in Patti's pocket, Chicky never got tired of the training game. Patti tried first one idea, then another, then another. She watched her chicken's responses carefully, as Mr. Wallace had said.

Chickens are naturally dopey in the dark, so Patti always saved the falcon hood till just before her bedtime. Then she could easily slip a hand–stitched piece of black velvet over Chicky's quietly murmuring head. Next morning, she would gently nudge the chicken on her breastbone until first one claw, then another, lifted to perch trustingly on Patti's wrist. She carried Chicky outside, slipped the hood off and watched her blink into the morning light.

"Br . . . awk!" is what Chicky always said before she jumped eagerly down to her dish of food.

Training Chicky was easy, but deciding on a good costume for herself was not. Patti spent hours with Mr.

Wallace's library book. How she would love to be perched sidesaddle on a horse—or on Sylvia's pony—resplendent in a richly trimmed cape. She giggled at the thought of the crowd's reaction to such a noble figure carrying a barnyard chicken.

But, after all, she concluded, it was probably a *farmer* who did the work of catching and training even the proudest and fiercest hawks. It was certainly an ordinary person who trained and cared for the horses. Probably the farmer's children helped him. And she, Patti, was a farmer's child. That's probably why it was the pictures of ordinary people that attracted Patti whenever she picked up Mr. Wallace's library book. She liked to look at the simple houses, the fields and hedgerows and imagine life as it might have been for a ten-year-old like herself.

The costume solution came as she poked around in the attic, just a week before the Fair. Earlier, she had found an old red summer skirt of Mom's that dropped right down to her bare feet. Then she found a stained white tablecloth with a lacey fringe that made an excellent shawl. It tucked into a belt in the front to hide her shirt.

That left just one last problem: it seemed that every little girl in the illustrations wore a white cap perched on the top of her long hair. Yuck! thought Patti. How they must have hated those caps—even more than the long skirts. How could they ever have had any fun without losing the silly things? More than anything, they looked like crocheted doilies—the kind her grandmother still used to cover the arms of her best living-room chairs.

Doilies. The problem was solved. Just a few minutes before, she had come across one of Gramma's doilies—probably one she made years before and sent to Mom as a gift. It was a big round one, meant for a table centre. But Mom wasn't a doily kind of person; so, here it was, folded up in the bottom of the big trunk. She could thread a length of elastic through the holes, and presto! a cap. Some of Mom's bobby pins would hold it firmly to her bouncy curls.

"Haven't you forgotten about Chicky?" asked Dad, early in the morning of the Fall Fair. He and Patti had just loaded Buttercup into the back of the pickup. Mom came out of the house and put her basket of lunch bags on the ground so she could lock the door. She looked around for Jamie, who was just bringing Goldy back from a quick run—it would be a long, lonely day for the dog, shut up in the kitchen. But no one in the family had any doubt that she would rather stay at home than risk another visit to the Fair.

"I was planning to come back for Chicky later," answered Patti mysteriously. "Can I put my bike in the pickup?"

"I suppose so . . ." said Dad. "It's not really very far for you to pedal, I guess. We'll strap it to the tailgate so it doesn't get in Buttercup's way."

And then he laughed.

"I think Patti *can* keep a secret, after all!" he announced, as the four of them crowded into the cab of the truck, with Patti perched on Mom's lap. "Does anyone else know what she and her chicken are up to?"

"I bet *I* know," said Jamie.

"Oh, no, you don't," declared Patti. "You couldn't possibly."

"Well, we'll all find out soon enough," said Mom, hugging Patti. "It starts at ten-thirty, doesn't it? Have you got everything ready?"

"Oh, sure," said Patti airily.

But time turned out to be rather short that morning, in spite of all Patti's planning. She hadn't lingered by the cow and calf pens as usual or played through the fence with the little goats. She hadn't entered anything in the baking class or drawn a picture or written a poem for the children's section—so she skipped her usual visit to the main building. Yet it seemed to take far too long to unload the cow and make the usual meeting arrangements with Mom and Dad. Then she had to look for Sylvia, who was braiding her pony's mane in a wooded hollow near the horse ring.

After a deep discussion with her friend, Patti dug out a small package from her pocket, and the two girls made a bargain.

The mile and a half both ways to the school property, which doubled as fair grounds once a year, seemed twice as far as usual. The September morning was hot, and she was in such a hurry. It was almost ten-thirty by the time Patti panted up the final hill, standing up on her pedals; she wheeled her bike behind a grove of trees, close to the fenced enclosure for the pet class. A large crowd had already gathered. Had she missed the start of the parade? Too early would spoil things—but so would too late.

Quickly Patti lifted a hooded and murmuring Chicky out of the box in her basket, then lowered her bike to the ground. She pulled the red skirt out from its bunching around the waist of her shorts and tossed her running shoes into her bike basket beside the lunch bag. Was her doily cap still there? Patti checked it with her free hand.

Carefully she balanced Chicky on her left wrist, and sighed with relief as the chicken, feeling the familiar perch, grasped it confidently with her long toes and stood up proudly—not at all like the uncertain, crouching position she had settled into during her long ride in the bicycle basket. Thank goodness Patti had practised that ride so many times before.

She paused for another moment behind the shelter of the trees to have a good look at Chicky. Around each yellow leg was a leather circlet; hooked to one of these was Goldy's old leash, which draped down across Patti's long skirt, then looped back up into her right hand. On Chicky's head was the black velvet hood which turned day into night, as far as the chicken was concerned.

Chicky wasn't afraid—she knew that all she had to do was to grip Patti's wrist until the night suddenly disappeared . . . and then it would be time to eat. She stood, her feathers a smooth, rippling brown, as tall and sure of herself as any falcon in a medieval picture.

Nothing changed Chicky's proud stance on Patti's wrist. Not Patti's stumbling walk through the tussocky grass in her bare feet, nor her awkward manoeuvring through the lines of people. Not even the short run at the last minute that brought Patti, puffing, to the end of the parade that was already beginning to move.

Perfect, so far.

Patti took a moment, as she walked, to check the faces that lined the fence. There were Mom and Dad, pointing and laughing—they had spotted her already. She grinned back at them, then continued her search. Jamie was with a bunch of his friends, but he hadn't seen her yet. Ah . . . *there* was Sylvia. She was hard to see at first, because she was crouching among the legs of the front row people along the farthest side of the ring. Relieved, Patti grinned at her. Now everything was ready.

Suddenly the crowd began to notice Patti and Chicky. They were at the end of a line of children leading dogs or carrying cats or little cages of gerbils or birds, rabbits or mice. There was nudging and laughter and the same comments over and over as the parade walked around the circle: "What *is* it?"

"I don't know. Why, it's . . . it's a *chicken!*"

Patti giggled to herself. This was more fun than she had ever imagined. Good old Chicky.

Just as she had hoped, she and Chicky were last out of the ring, so when they and the whole column of children turned around, they were first in line to do their demonstration. Thank goodness you could count on the judges to do things the same way year after year.

Patti strode out into the middle of the ring with Chicky held high in front of her.

"What's she gonna *do?*" piped a small voice in the crowd.

Patti glanced over at her friend, saw her raise her arm and send a small, grey object flying through the air. It landed close to Patti's feet. It was a cloth rabbit. Suddenly it began to move, very slowly, pulled by a string that lay along the top of the stubbly grass.

This was the moment. Off came Chicky's black hood. Quickly Patti unhooked the leash.

"Ba . . . awk!" said the chicken, blinking in the sunlight. The crowd burst into laughter.

But Chicky paid no attention. She knew what to do. There, that thing moving through the grass—*that's* what she had been waiting for all morning.

Chicky leapt from Patti's hand, fluttered to the ground and pounced on the rabbit. With her sharp leathery nails and pointed beak she pecked at the woolly material until a hole appeared—and a stream of oats.

Hoots of laughter and a great round of applause cheered Patti, the trainer and Chicky, her clever falcon.

Later, as Patti stood on a stump near the edge of the clearing to watch Sylvia ride in her pony class, she was surprised to see Dad walk around the outside of the crowd, peering here and there. He was looking for her.

"Over here, Dad," she mouthed, waving wildly. She didn't want to make a noise and interrupt the concentration of the riders and the spectators.

"What are you doing so far away from the ring?" he asked in a stage whisper.

"I'm Sylvia's groom today," she whispered back, looking down at him from her perch on the stump. "It's a bargain we made. I'm keeping the water bucket filled and brushing the pony for her. I stayed with him when she went for lunch, too. Sylvia showed me how to clean his feet today."

"I see." Dad grinned up at her. "A pretty good day, all in all, eh? Though I must say, Chicky looked as happy as the cow to get back home again. *She* didn't seem particularly impressed by the blue rosette on her cardboard box. Did you remember to explain to her what *first place* means?"

They were interrupted by a sudden round of applause from the people around the ring.

"Look," Patti pointed. "It's Sylvia's turn to canter now. She's been having a hard time getting her pony to lead on the proper leg."

"How is she doing?" asked Dad quietly. He couldn't see very well over the heads of the crowd.

"I don't know," confessed Patti. "I haven't learned to tell the difference yet."

But a burst of clapping from the crowd answered their question for them.

Dad shook his head in wonder as everyone around them began to talk and laugh, and the horses lined up to leave the ring.

"It's amazing when you think of it," he said. "The complicated things that animals can be taught to do."

"It isn't really the animals that get trained," explained Patti. "It just looks that way. Mostly, it's the *people* who get trained."

Dad looked up at her, puzzled.

"Mr. Wallace told me that," she said, looking down at her father's tanned face and fly-away hair. It always surprised her when she discovered there were things he didn't know.

Playhouse

PATTI CROUCHED, HER FACE CLOSE TO THE LOG; she watched the dragon pull itself slowly over crusty bark. Armour a shiny black. Huge goggles. Or maybe that was a helmet, not goggles. It looked *so* tired. Did it even care that there was a spy so near? Turquoise wings shimmered in the afternoon light.

But now Patti could see there was something seriously wrong with one of the wings. She poked her head up cautiously for a better look. Yes, the second one on the far side was torn; it lay awkwardly across the first. The other wings looked battered too. It was nothing but an old dragonfly now, silhouetted against the blue October sky. As it dragged its hind end along the log, the tough scales rasped like paper. She wondered where it was going. Where *could* it go, now that summer was over?

Sighing, she got up from behind the log and reached for her stick broom. She could at least finish sweeping the dirt floor of her little living room while she waited for Joan. Maybe she should fix the broom too—it still worked pretty well, but the string that tied the bundle of twigs to the stick was getting loose. Patti pushed on it irritably, so she could watch it wobble. She just wanted to play house today, but nothing seemed to be going right.

Warm sun pushed its way through the yellow alder leaves, splashing a golden light over the table and Patti's tea things. She had the crackers and cheese out already, the milk in the jug, the tea in the teapot, the cookies on a plate. But where was Joan? This always seemed to happen. How could they ever play together if Joan was always goofing off alone among the trees, exploring or doing whatever she did all the time?

"Drop your weapons—you're surrounded!"

Patti jumped as the raspy voice boomed from behind the bushes. Then, with a laugh of relief, she obediently let her broom fall and raised her hands above her head.

"Mercy!" she cried. "Don't kill me and my babies. I'll give you all our gold. And feed you."

A tall, tanned girl slipped out from behind a nearby tree, waving a large bow made of an alder stick and string.

"Sorry I took so long," she said. "Mom needed me. And I have to go back in a few minutes."

She sat down on a round of wood next to the square of old plywood that served as their table, and tossed her bow and arrow into a patch of grass.

Disappointment had replaced the laughter on Patti's face.

"But you promised to play house with me today," she protested. "Remember? I was the crew of your ship yesterday. And I've had everything ready for ages."

"Sorry," said Joan. She lifted one of the tiny blue china cups and looked at the rose painted on its side. "Where did you get these?" she asked, changing the subject. "Are they your mom's?"

"No," said Patti, squatting down beside the table—there was only one chair—and pouring a dollop of the sweet cold tea into each cup. "My gramma gave them to me. My last birthday. They were hers—although Mom used to play with them too."

"What's wrong?" Patti asked sharply, then. She didn't like the closed look that sometimes appeared on Joan's face. "Is there something wrong with getting a tea set from my gram?"

"Can't stay," said Joan abruptly, reaching for a cracker and standing up so suddenly she bumped the table which was balanced precariously on a stump.

"Watch it!" Patti grabbed the plywood just in time to

stop the tea set from slipping off. "It isn't fair," she said indignantly, freckles beginning to pop out on her flushed face.

Joan hesitated for a moment. "You want to come too?" she asked.

"What—to your house?" said Patti. She was surprised right out of her anger by the invitation. She had never been to the faded grey house at the crossroads halfway to town, although Joan and her family had moved there way back last spring and the two girls had been friends ever since. They played together either at school or at Patti's. She had seen the baby and the other two little ones in her family, but only from a distance as she rode by on her bike and waved to Joan, standing beside the old rope swing.

"Sure, I guess," Patti said thoughtfully. "We could go up to my house and leave a note for Mom, in case she gets home before I do."

"Do you really *want* to?" asked Joan. "You don't have to, you know. I might be able to come back here later."

Patti considered.

"I'd like to meet your family," she said.

They rode phantom horses back down the lane from the house, Patti leading for once: this was something she could do every bit as well as Joan. Through the woods they galloped wildly, jumping old branches, puddles, clumps of fallen leaves. Then along the side of Mr. Hardy's field, behind the gravel pit, over the dirt road and into the woods on the other side.

"You promised! Push me, Joanie." The small face on the swing was brown like Joan's, the eyes large and black, the dark hair tousled. He looked about five, Patti guessed.

"In a second, Alec."

A little girl in braids had turned from her play in time to see Patti and Joan bursting out of the shortcut through the woods. With a happy screech she ran to them now, arms extended, and hurled herself at Joan's knees. She looked up at Patti through her bangs and stuck like a leech to her big sister.

"Hi, Emmy," Joan said absently, as she unfastened the small wiry body enough to continue her walk to the house. But the instant she slowed, the little girl wrapped herself tightly around Joan again.

Patti felt strange—as if she had landed suddenly in a foreign country. Or a dream. It seemed that Joan had been transformed into someone different at the exact moment they left the path in the bushes and entered the dusty, summer-beaten yard. No longer was she an adventurer, plunging through the forest on the trail of a gang of bandits. Or a highwayman capturing gold. In one practised movement, Joan pulled a Kleenex from her back pocket to wipe the nose of the little girl attached to her legs; then she reached over and scooped up a brown baby sitting in the dooryard, nibbling at a handful of dirt with an air of intense concentration.

"Are you there, Joanie?" A voice emerged faintly through the ragged screen door.

"I'm back, Mom," called Joan. She looked quickly at Patti as she unwrapped the little girl from her legs once more and pulled the door open with the hand still holding the baby.

"Could you wait here for just a minute?"

Joan, the pirate, had never looked at Patti quite like that before—anxious, almost pleading. She held the door open for her little sister and let it slam shut behind them. A stale smell of kitchen and cigarettes escaped in a puff of air. Patti waited in the sunshine. She looked over at the road, the crossroads that she had walked or biked or bused past practically every day of her life. It looked so different now, from here, the back door of Joan's house. And the yard that had always seemed smooth and grassy turned out to be not like that at all. Instead, it was just a lot of little bumps and tussocks of dandelions and weeds surrounded by hard, bare ground. In the dust at her feet lay two toy cars and a faded plastic shovel that had once been red.

A creaking noise reminded her that she wasn't alone. She looked up to see Alec busy twisting the swing he was sitting on. Around and around he pushed himself, his sneakers braced against the release of the spin before he was ready. The rope above him was wound about as tight as he could make it, and his short legs hardly touched the ground any more. But still he twisted, slowly, patiently, until the rope above him bumped out into knots. Only the small of his back was still connected to the wooden seat now. Each time he came around, his eyes flicked to Patti, and there they stuck for as long as his circle would allow it. Then around he came again, his eyes darting back to her. At last he stopped. He checked once more—was Patti still watching? Then he stretched with all his might to get a good toe purchase on the ground, and he pushed.

Wildly the swing spun—back and forth and around like a top. Alec's face was a silent blur. In a matter of seconds it was over. Patti watched as the little boy sat motionless, staring at his shoes long after the swing had come to a stop. Finally, he looked up again at Patti.

"C'mon in, Patti." Joan's voice startled her through the screen. Her friend's face, and the baby in her arms, seemed white against the indoor shadows.

"Mom wants to see you," murmured Joan as Patti stepped in from the sunshine. The door swung shut behind them.

It took a moment for Patti's eyes to get used to the gloom. When at last she could see the very large woman sitting in a wooden chair by the table, Patti realized that Joan's mom had been watching her ever since she stepped into the kitchen. She hesitated. Those eyes made her shy: she pulled back a little from Joan's guiding hand.

"I won't bite." The laugh that accompanied this decla-
ration was deep and throaty, and turned immediately into
a hacking cough that shook the woman's whole body. Patti
watched, astonished, as it wobbled like Jell-O. Her cheeks
trembled and so did her upper arms where they squeezed
out of the faded cotton dress. Against her enormous chest
she pressed two balloon hands, fingers spread wide as if to
hold together a loosely packed mountain of flesh. Suddenly Patti was afraid of what might happen. She looked
quickly for Joan, who was busy settling the baby on a blanket in the corner.

But now Joan was swinging her long legs over toys and
calmly disentangling a tall glass from the pile of dishes
stacked beside the sink. She ran the water for a moment,
and filled the glass. By the time she had set it on the table
in front of her mother, the coughing had subsided.
Another rumble or two, a gulp from the glass of water,
then the eyes turned outward again. Patti was once more
frozen in their unwelcome spotlight.

"C'mon over," Joan said to Patti, motioning impatiently
with her hand. As if nothing at all unusual had happened.

Patti crossed the bumpy linoleum floor and stood close
to her friend. There was a breadcrust on the table, she
noticed. A scattering of crumbs, a breadknife, an almost
empty ketchup bottle, a white mug with brown stains down
the inside, two overflowing ashtrays, a packet of cigarettes
with a yellow lighter on top.

"So this is Patti," said Joan's mom. There was a hint of laughter in the statement. It made Patti feel better all of a sudden; she smiled hesitantly at the face in front of her—so large and strange, and yet so familiar, because the eyes, deep and dark, were just like Joan's.

"Well, what do you think of me?"

Patti was shocked once more. Her smile vanished as quickly as it had come, her panic growing in the silence that filled the room. Was she really expected to *answer* that question?

"Patti and I have a house in the woods, Mom," interrupted Joan casually. She seemed unaware of any awkwardness as she wiped the table with a cloth from the sink, gathering up all the crumbs from between the various objects on the table. Patti had never seen Joan do such a thing before—mother-type jobs like this had always been left for Patti in their playhouse.

"Patti made a table and a chair for it—and she even made tea for us to drink. Everything's really pretty."

Patti was surprised to hear Joan talk about the playhouse so enthusiastically. They both knew perfectly well that Joan didn't really like playing house—she only put up with it so that Patti would agree to being burned at the stake or made to walk the plank. But Joan didn't return Patti's questioning look: she was concentrating on brushing all the collected crumbs carefully into her hand.

"That's nice," said Joan's mom, who was still watching

Patti. "I played games like that too, when I was small," she rumbled. "Do you have walls for your playhouse? Is it a real house?"

"No," Patti shook her head. Here was something she could talk about. "We just have a place among the trees," she explained, "—the bushes . . ."

But Patti's mom wasn't listening. She continued as if Patti hadn't spoken at all. "It's nice when you're a kid and can play all day. Like Emmy and the baby."

Patti followed her look to the corner by the front window where the baby sat on a blanket with a bottle dangling from her mouth, teeth clenched to hold the nipple. The baby was watching, entranced, as Emmy put on a silent performance.

Emmy's hair was pulled back tightly from her face into a topknot and the bib of her overalls hung so low around her waist that a pair of dingy underpants poked out each time she bent over. She was carefully lining up a row of small toys along the windowsill. Then she made a gun with her forefinger and whispered, "bang, bang!" swishing them all to the floor with a sudden sweep of her hand. A rubber chicken bounced and the baby gurgled with laughter. Grinning, the little girl bent to pick up the toys and start the game all over again.

"You live on the farm with the big red barn? Just beyond the gravel pit?" Joan's mom was back to asking questions.

Patti nodded.

"I'm having a bad spell today, ain't I, Joanie?" she said. "My heart is bad." This explanation was to Patti.

"Sure, Mom," answered Joan, matter-of-factly. "But you're feeling better now. You'll be all better soon."

"My heart is still thumping hard," complained Joan's mom. "You don't know how my heart is thumping. Why should you even care?"

This last comment was definitely a whine—at least that's what her mom called it, whenever Patti spoke that way. Patti had just had a very strange and shocking idea—that it was Joan who seemed to be the mother in this family.

"It'll be okay, Mom," soothed Joan. "Should I start peeling the potatoes now?"

"Joanie doesn't believe me," complained Joan's mom to Patti. "You can see for yourself. She doesn't believe me."

"Aw, Mom . . ." said Joan.

"Shut up!" This was loud. Startling. The subdued chatter of the little ones in the corner stopped. The dark eyes in the large, quivering face held Patti glued to her spot on the linoleum—Joan's mom expected an answer and Patti didn't know what to do. Suddenly, before she realized it was going to happen, the woman had reached to grab Patti's hand. She held it hard, too hard, buried in the dimpled flesh of both her own hands.

"C'mon," she said, pulling Patti towards her. Joan stepped out of the way and Patti stumbled closer to her friend's mother—closer than she wanted to be. There was a sharp smell of sweat and cigarettes. Her hand was pressed now against the woman's soft chest. It was sinking deeper and deeper into the faded cotton.

"Can you feel it?" The eyes, so close, large and incredibly deep.

"Can you *feel* it—my heart?" The voice insisted.

And now Patti *could* feel it—a firm thump against her fingers, as if some small creature was imprisoned. Smothered, like Patti's hand. Struggling to get away. It paused after each beat, hesitated for a moment, thumped again. The three hands, clasped together tightly, rose and fell gently, irregularly, with her breathing, and underneath it Patti could feel this thing, Joan's mother's heart. It seemed dangerous. Out of control. Who knew what it could do to all of them in this room? Patti wriggled her hand to free it, but Joan's mom held on.

"You feel it? It could stop any time," she said.

With a sudden wrench, Patti pulled her hand away and turned blindly towards the door. Then she remembered her manners.

"Thank you," she said breathlessly, turning, forcing herself to look up again at Joan's mom—at the large dark eyes. Then she looked away again quickly.

"See you at school," she muttered to Joan, her voice wobbly. She couldn't seem to get enough air.

Patti stood outside on the step for a moment after the

screen door had banged behind her. The sunshine and yellow leaves were too bright, too much of a glare.

She noticed that Joan's little brother, Alec, had wound his swing up again; he was ready for another spin. This time she didn't wait to watch him. Instead, she walked towards the crossroads, stumbling a little on the tussocky yard. She was puffing, as if she had run a long way, but of course she hadn't.

She slowed down when she reached the road. Then she stopped and put her hand tentatively to the left side of her chest. She could feel nothing at all. Where was it? She moved her hand closer to the centre, and there she found it—the steady thump, thump of her heart.

Patti ended up jogging most of the way home, but twice before she got there, she stopped and checked once more for the elusive beat of her heart. It seemed such a gentle thing, so fragile. She hadn't realized, before now, how much depended on it.

Making Muscles

THE TREE LIGHTS TWINKLED IN THE CORNER. Patti lay on the carpet beside the wood heater in her pyjamas, reading her new Nancy Drew detective book. The brightness in the room came from outside, from the fine dusting of snow two days ago, a Christmas wish come true.

The stove was lit in the living room because it was Christmas holidays. The usual winter weekday routine of living mostly in the kitchen—running through the hall, down the stairs, and slamming the kitchen door tight against the dark, damp chill of the rest of the house—all that had been put aside, along with other ordinary things.

Like school. And Mom and Dad going to work. It was like ten Sundays in a row.

It must be almost lunchtime, Patti thought—she could hear Dad, back from the barn chores already, talking to Mom in the kitchen.

"No, I don't think she's too young," Mom was saying, her voice carrying clearly through the open door. "I'll come out and teach her, though, so it doesn't slow down your chores."

Patti sat up to listen.

"Her hands aren't as big as Jamie's were at that age, that's what's worrying me," Dad said. "That could make it harder."

What were they talking about?

Patti scrambled to her feet. Should she listen at the door? That's how Nancy Drew found out about important things.

"Is it about me?" Darn. She had burst through the doorway before she remembered to try eavesdropping.

Dad looked startled for a moment. He was sitting at the table with a cup of coffee. Mom laughed.

"It sure is," she said, turning from a steaming pot of soup on the stove to look at Patti. "It's about learning to milk the cows. What do you think about that idea?"

"Oh, yeah!" exclaimed Patti, looking from one grinning face to the other. "You mean, right now?"

"We'll start tonight," Mom promised. "After Jamie leaves on his Scout trip. We'll do Buttercup for the rest of the holidays, you and I, and let Dad do the other two cows. Okay, Bob? That'll be a bit of a help, anyway."

"Sounds good," Dad agreed. He reached out for Patti.

"Let's have a look at those hands," he said. "Hmm." He looked up doubtfully at Patti's face, then brushed a straggle of hair away from her forehead.

"Don't worry if you don't catch on too quickly, Pats. It takes a lot of hand muscle to milk a cow, and yours are still pretty small."

Patti pulled her hands away from Dad and looked at them critically.

"They're okay," she said. "It'll be all right."

It was a worry, though. She collected her clothes from her bedroom and wandered past Jamie's partly open door into the bathroom to dress over the iron grille that piped the warm air up from the kitchen stove. And then she remembered something: Jamie still had the set of barbells in his room—the ones he had borrowed from his friend Pete last fall. Patti knew he exercised with them every night before he went to bed. He was working on his muscles, though he refused to explain exactly why.

"Go away!" was what he said the last time she asked. He looked angry and embarrassed. She knew he would be furious if she touched those barbells. They were more special than any of the other things in his room. More special, even, than his fishing rod, hanging on the wall.

But Jamie was away at a meeting of his Scout troop; the

boys were wrapping the wooden bookends they had made as gifts for the families they would stay with in the city. He had been excited about this adventure for a long time— about the friends he would make and the museums he would visit. And swimming in the YMCA pool. He wasn't likely to be thinking about Pete's barbells.

Patti put her ear against the grille at her feet: Mom's and Dad's voices were still buzzing down in the kitchen. Good. Because she was going to make muscles while Jamie was away. After all, it wasn't as if you could *hurt* silly old barbells.

Quickly Patti tossed her pyjamas into her bedroom and slipped sideways through the partly open door into Jamie's room. His suitcase was open on the bed; it had been packed since last night and the room was strangely tidy. She could even see the barbells on the closet floor beside a row of shoes, not buried, as usual, under a mound of T-shirts and underwear.

There was a metal rod you were supposed to lift, and on either end were clipped the weights you added as you got stronger. She could see that there were two discs on each end already, and that the others lay in a pile in the back corner. Patti listened first for sounds from down-stairs, then she knelt in the closet doorway and gripped the bar in both hands. Leaning back and bracing her shoulders, she tried to lift the bar. And she could. As high as her chest, anyway.

Gently she laid the bar back on the floor. Whew! She breathed in and out, stretching her hands and rubbing out the strain. She certainly couldn't raise the weight above her shoulders, like Jamie. But that didn't matter, did it? It was her *hands* that needed the muscle for milking, not her arms. And they needed that muscle right away. For tonight.

She reached for the bar again, lifted it as high as she could, held it there until her arms began to shake; then she put it back down carefully. Again she did it. And again. The back door slammed. She paused, startled. But the house was quiet once more.

She rubbed her hands. They were getting sore, and so were her forearms. But that was good—it meant the bars were making muscle. Anyway, that's what Jamie always said: it had to hurt to make muscle.

Patti replaced the barbells exactly as she had found them and hurried downstairs. Right after lunch, she was going to town with Dad, so she could spend the afternoon with her friend Ruth. But first, there was something she wanted to do.

It was a grey, cold day, and the wind whipped around Mom's little red roadster—that's what they called a car in the Nancy Drew books. A roadster. Patti said the word over in her mind as she struggled with the heavy bar on the barn door. Inside, it was warm, quiet and mysterious. This was Patti's favourite place in the winter—the dim centre bay was full of the summer smell of hay bales stacked around the windows in the loft above her. Spider webs, decorated with bits of chaff and old fly bodies, were lit by the columns of light shafting down to the main floor.

From the stalls she could hear the constant munching of Celeste, the Holstein cow. Patti peered over the gate at her black-and-white rump. Next came Buttercup—the oldest of the two Jerseys—who turned her beautiful dark dish face to inspect Patti for a moment, then reached into her manger for another mouthful of the hay Dad had put there a short while before. In the stall next to her was Daisy, her calf of two summers ago, who now had her own calf beside her. Only Dad could coax Daisy to let him milk her for a few minutes every day.

When there was snow, the cows spent most of their days and nights in their stalls instead of out in the field. Patti liked to visit them there, swinging on their gates and watching them close up. She loved their milky smell and the sound of their stomachs rumbling, the whirl of their short hair around their bony haunches, the peaceful rhythms as they chewed their cuds.

"I'm going to milk you tonight," Patti suddenly said out loud to Buttercup. She covered her mouth in dismay as her voice echoed from the dark corners. She didn't talk out loud to the cows any more—not since she was a little kid. What would detective Nancy think of such a thing? What would *Jamie* say?

Later that evening, she realized how lucky it was that her brother would be away for a whole week. She would need all that time to be good at milking before he came home. Perched on the old wooden milking stool in the barn, her face was close to the warmth of Buttercup's golden white belly. Mom squatted beside her, reaching out to adjust Patti's awkward fingers around two of the soft wrinkled teats. Patti's hands had been getting stiffer since the morning, even while she played hide-and-seek in the hallways of Ruth's old farmhouse, then persuaded her friend to practise arm wrestling at the kitchen table.

"I need to get my hands strong for milking," she had explained. She didn't tell Ruth about the barbells.

"You're learning to milk?" Ruth's freckled face showed she was impressed. But her long arms had beaten Patti every time.

"Let's go sleighing," she suggested finally, as Patti's shoulders slumped in discouragement.

Back home, after the family had waved goodbye to Jamie, Patti struggled awkwardly with the forks and knives as she set the table for supper. She had never been so aware of her hands and fingers and wrists, or had had so much trouble getting them to do what she wanted. Making muscle was a painful business.

Now, in the dim light of the barn, she gritted her teeth with the effort of milking—tightening the forefinger and thumb of her right hand, squeezing the next fingers against the palm of her hand the way Mom showed her. At last! A thin stream of milk in the bucket. But, oh, it was *so* much harder than it looked.

"Good," said Mom. "you're getting it. Now try the other hand."

Ten minutes later, there was scarcely enough milk to cover the bottom of the bucket, and Buttercup was beginning to stamp her feet.

"That's a good start," Mom said. "I'll finish tonight, and we'll try again tomorrow."

Patti got up off the stool reluctantly.

"Do you think my hands will ever get strong enough?" she asked.

"Definitely," promised Mom, as streams of milk sang into the pail between her knees. "It's just a matter of exercise. I've been doing this for a lot of years, don't forget."

Exercise. Patti walked through the winter darkness to the kitchen to put out the strainer and the milk bottles, ready for Mom and Dad. The trouble is, I haven't done enough exercise yet, she decided. I've just got to be better at milking tomorrow. What if, when Jamie came home at the end of the week, she *still* couldn't milk Buttercup?

She ran up the shadowy stairs, reaching automatically for the light switch in Jamie's room. No. Not a good idea. A light in her brother's window might be hard to explain. But it was very dark in the bedroom, with just a pale reflection from the stars and snow framed by the window.

And it was pitch black in the corner by the closet. Patti knelt, feeling along the floor for Jamie's shoes, his gym bag. Ah! That must be the barbells.

Hurry! Mom and Dad would get back from the barn any minute now. She grabbed the bar with both hands, lifting it towards her. Ouch! With a clatter the weights hit the closet floor. Patti cradled her right hand in her left against her chest. "Ow!" She whispered it. "Ow!" The house was quiet. No one had heard the noise. In the dark, muffled closet, the barbells lay silent. She must have picked them up too close to one end. Unbalanced them. She had twisted and wrenched her wrist and hand.

Cold water. That's what she needed now. Patti stumbled to the bathroom to fill the sink. In a few minutes her throbbing hand felt blessedly numb from the cold. How long could she stay here before her parents noticed? She heard the kitchen door open downstairs.

"Patti? You there?" It was Mom.

"Just up in the bathroom," Patti called. Good. She had made her voice sound matter-of-fact. Normal.

Now what? If only she could stay up here for the evening, so she didn't have to explain her sore hand. What she needed was a good excuse. Alibi: that was the right word.

"I'm going to read in bed now, Mom." She ran and leaned over the balcony to announce this, as casually as she could.

"My new Nancy Drew book," she added.

"Okay, honey."

Did Mom sound a bit surprised? Ah, good—the back door was opening again. Dad's voice. The sounds of milk pouring. The news suddenly blaring on the radio.

One-handed, she brushed her teeth and wriggled into her pyjamas and under her covers. Then came another struggle—somehow she had to balance her new book on top of the quilt and still snuggle as far under as possible. Patti sighed with frustration. It was hard to concentrate on reading. Her good arm was cold because it was out of the covers, and her hurt hand was throbbing again. Who would be so stupid as to read in bed in a cold bedroom in the winter? No wonder Mom had sounded surprised.

Patti pictured the warm stove down in the living room, Mom reading or knitting, Dad with the newspaper. The end of the next sigh became a gulp, almost a sob—her hand was so sore, and she couldn't even talk to her parents about it. They would probably tell Jamie. And he would be furious if he knew she had used the borrowed barbells.

Read, Patti told herself. Nancy Drew and her friends were creeping up to the house where the smugglers had hidden the loot. Were the smugglers still there? Would Nancy get caught? Patti wiped at her cheek with her shoulder; the tears were beginning to blur the print.

She pulled her right hand out from under the covers to look at it. It was beginning to swell now; it was especially tight and shiny around her thumb. She probably needed a bandage on it. Oh, couldn't she manage without a bandage for just one night?

But . . . but what would she tell Mom and Dad tomorrow, when it came time for milking and they saw her hand? There *must* be a way she could keep those barbells a secret. Think of all the secrets detective Nancy managed to keep. In every chapter of every book.

Gee, she could maybe say to her parents—so surprised—I don't know *how* I hurt my hand!

No. That wouldn't work at all. Dad would naturally jump to the conclusion that she wasn't strong enough to start milking yet—because, if she didn't tell the truth, he would guess it was milking Buttercup that had hurt her hand. Then they would make her wait for another whole year.

"Oh-h-h," groaned Patti, pulling both arms back under the covers.

Nancy Drew flipped shut and slid off her knees and on to the floor with a thump.

Patti sighed a last sigh. Then she crawled out of bed and reached for her dressing gown and slippers. She turned on the light over the stairs, and headed down to Mom and Dad in the warm living room. To heck with secrets, she had decided. Nancy Drew could keep them if she liked. In real life, they seemed to be a lot more trouble than they were worth.

Freeze-up

"Everything's frozen solid out there," Jamie announced through Patti's open bedroom door.

"Does that mean we can make the rink today?" Patti came up out of her dreams quickly. There was excitement in Jamie's voice.

"I'm going to ask Dad right now," said Jamie. "He said we could do it as soon as everything freezes up hard."

Patti knelt on her bed, pulling the curtain aside so she could see for herself what the weather was like. It was grey and cloudy; the few brown leaves left on the large maples along the road flapped crisply in the wind. A fine white powder skittered along the top of a foot and a half of snow on the ground. There were frost flowers lining her window this morning—in a few days she wouldn't be able to see outside at all, until she had melted round peepholes with her breath.

Patti shivered and let the curtain drop as she snuggled back under her quilts. Then she remembered the rink. In a moment she was up on her knees again, holding the curtain out of the way. Just below her window was the field they had chosen for it. It was close to the house, the wire fence running just a few feet from the kitchen window. This was important to their planning because, as Jamie had pointed out, the light from the kitchen would allow them to skate after dark. His friend Pete had electric lights strung out to their rink last year, but Jamie and Patti both knew their dad wouldn't even consider the extra expense.

"What's wrong with skating in the daylight?" That's what he would say to such an idea.

But he had approved of making the rink in that field, for a different reason.

"It'll be easy to slip the wire off the fence right there so we can get through," he said. "And it's close to the house for hauling the buckets. A rink, even a small one, will take a lot of water."

He had offered to help them with it, if they would wait till after Christmas for hard freeze-up. He didn't want to go to all that work just to have it thaw again. Dad didn't have much time for such things these days: even in the winter there was a lot of work waiting to be done on the farm, since he was away working in the mill every week-day, and it was dark by the time he got home.

But today was Sunday. Patti peeled off her pyjamas, grabbed her jogging pants and wool socks and headed for the warm-air vent in the bathroom. She could smell coffee as she darted through the chilly hallway.

"I'm sorry, Jamie," Dad was saying as Patti burst, at last, through the kitchen door.

It was bright and warm in the kitchen. But Jamie looked gloomy in spite of that, and in spite of the pan-cakes piled high on his plate. Dad had his mouth in the firm line that suggested a decision even *he* wasn't happy about.

"Shut the door, Patti," said her mother as she flipped more pancakes.

"Can't we do the rink today, then?" asked Patti, guess-ing the cause of the gloom.

"I've simply *got* to finish the inside of the barn today, Patti," said Dad. "And I need the daylight to be sure I've found all the holes—I thought I'd blocked every one of them after that dratted mink last June. But a weasel's killed a lot of our pullets in the last couple of weeks, and we'll lose the laying chickens, too, if I don't get on to it right away. Besides, it's too cold in there now, with the old planks stripped off—if we want eggs, I've got to get the insulation in right away. And the inside wall finished."

"What if the kids and I give you a hand with it?" suggested Mom. "Maybe we could get it done in time to start the rink today."

"I thought you were busy with a lunch social after church," Dad said.

"Oh, I don't mind giving that up for once," said Mom, putting a heaping platter on the table before she sat down.

"Especially if I knew it would make a difference," she added.

Dad looked thoughtful.

"Are you sure?" he asked. "This is your one time of the week to see your friends." Mom was the only one who went to church on ordinary Sundays.

Mom smiled and nodded.

"Well, it *would* help," he said slowly. "I don't like to ask Maynard to give up his only day off—but someone holding and fetching and so on would sure make my work go faster. If we all worked all afternoon . . . well, we might finish by supper time."

"But then we still wouldn't have time to do the rink today," Jamie pointed out crossly.

"No," said Dad. "Not today. But I would be free to start it when I got home after work tomorrow."

"It'll be dark, remember?" said Jamie.

Dad laughed. He put a hand on his son's shoulder.

"What about the light from the kitchen window?" he

pointed out. "If you can use that light for skating on the rink, you can surely use it for *making* it."

Next day, Patti hurried home from school in the winter dusk, her head hunched down inside her red wool scarf. It was cold and still. No wind, and that's good if you want ice to freeze nice and smooth, she was thinking as she walked. Dad and Jamie had discussed the details last night.

As soon as she got home—too bad it was basketball today, and she'd had to miss the school bus—she would help Jamie walk the outside boundary of the rink. Then they would get a couple of smallish pieces of plywood from the barn and jump on them to tamp down the snow inside the outline. By the time Dad got home, the snow would be packed as hard as they could make it, and they could start hauling water.

"Just don't make it too big," Dad had warned Jamie. "You have no idea how much water it'll take."

Patti began to jog a little, her breath a cloud, puffing through the holes in the scarf, making it damp and itchy on the inside. Jamie would have started already, she knew. She hoped it didn't have to be *too* small. It would be nice if it could be *almost* as big as the one Pete and his dad made last year.

A commotion interrupted her thoughts. It came from over the field to her right. Squinting into the grey-blue light, she could just make out a pack of dogs, as they circled and yipped and milled about.

What on earth was going on?

Now they began to spread out, heading for the open gate next to the road at the top of the hill. She knew that black lab that led the line-up—he came from a farm over the way. And the yellow long-haired dog belonged to her friend Deirdre's family. She didn't know the others. There were five or six of them. What were they doing?

As they raced across the snowy field towards the road, Patti suddenly realized that Bonkers, the black dog, wasn't at the very front of the pack after all. Zipping along, low to the ground in front of him, was a small, beige-coloured runty kind of dog—like a chihuahua, only bigger and stubbier. Ignoring the open gate, it slipped under a gap in the fence that was too small for the bigger dogs behind. As it darted across the road in front of her, Patti gasped to see that blood streaked its face and along its side and back.

By now, the chasing dogs had swerved to go through the gate, and the runty dog had disappeared over the edge into the gravel pit to the left of the road. In a moment they were all gone, leaving nothing but a trail of excited yapping in the crisp evening air.

Patti stood, stunned. The big dogs were all after the small one. And it was hurt already. A whole pack of big dogs against one little dog. It wasn't fair! What were they going to do to it?

Patti began to run. In a second she was through the hard-packed bank left by the snow-plough, and into the softer snow on the side road that led to the gravel pit. She couldn't go as fast as the dogs, especially since she had left her laces flapping—the snow pulled at her boots with every step.

By the time she reached the edge of the pit, it was too shadowy to see into it very well. But she could hear the yipping of the pack from across the other side. She scanned the cliffside, each patch of gleam and shadow made by the scrubby trees, each outcrop of rock with its little hat of snow.

As her eyes became accustomed to the dim light, she spotted the movement of the dogs, all crowded together on a ledge halfway up the opposite slope. They were an ever-shifting clump of bodies—first one was on top, then another—and their baying had become a strange, howling noise that echoed off the sides of the pit. The cold crept into Patti's down jacket; she shivered. She noticed that, in spite of their constant milling and confusion, each dog's attention remained focused on the same spot, directly above their own small ledge.

At last Patti could see what they were looking at. The little dog's dingy coat blended with the dusk—it was the whites of its eyes that gave it away. It crouched against the cliff wall, against a small evergreen tree clinging to the precipice.

Patti wondered how the little creature had managed to get up there. The other dogs certainly couldn't, and they were definitely frustrated. As Patti watched, one after another, they hurled themselves against the bank, then fell back. Now it was Bonkers's turn. Frantic, his forepaws as high as he could reach on the slippery snow, he strained his neck and howled angrily at the dark sky. He was no more than a few feet from his prey. Again and again, each of the dogs made a run at the slope, then slipped back into the turmoil below.

Patti was glad to see that a black-and-white collie missed its footing entirely after one of these attempts. It tumbled, head over tail, down into the gravel pit below. Soundlessly it rolled. When it hit the bottom, it stood for a moment, then shook a fine cloud of snow into the darkness. Then it turned and zigzagged up the roadway, a grey shadow hugging the ground. Alarmed, Patti saw that it wasn't heading back up to the other dogs, but around to the top of the pit opposite her. Right above the little dog huddled in the snow.

"Oh, no," gasped Patti. "Go home!" she shrilled into the gathering darkness. "Go home, all of you! Go on! Get out of it!" She was screaming now, her voice breaking.

But the dogs didn't seem to hear her, although their yipping and howling had stopped. They were watching the collie.

Back and forth along the cliff top it raced, nose to the ground. It was looking for the way down. Already it had its forepaws onto a possible ledge and was hunting for another foothold.

As if on a signal the pack moved all at once—hurling themselves down the slope as the collie had done. They lunged, rolled and slid down the steep cliff.

Patti didn't wait to see what happened next. She had to get help. Quickly. As the first dog picked itself up at the bottom, Patti ran to the fence that separated the gravel-pit field from their own hay field.

Desperately, she searched for a way over the wire. She knew there was one farther down near the woods, where a tree had fallen up against the fence. But she didn't have time to run that far.

She threw her book pack over the fence and did what her dad had warned her she mustn't do: using the wire squares like rungs on a ladder, she pulled herself up next to the fence post. The wire creaked and the old post groaned as it leaned towards her, leaving her hanging almost horizontal to the snow. Puffing, she managed to twist herself and swing her bulky snow pants, first one leg then the other, over the fence. She wobbled for a moment near the top of the wire, then jumped free.

The renewed yelping of the dogs faded behind her as she concentrated on taking big steps, so her boots wouldn't pull off as often. The kitchen light was on already. And there was Jamie, pacing back and forth, working on their rink.

She stood for a moment, out of breath. "Jamie!" she called.

He looked up and waved to her.

"Jamie! Come quickly!" she yelled, beckoning with her mittened hand.

He looked at her for a moment, appearing puzzled. Then he shook his head and beckoned back to her. He began once again to make big steps in the snow.

Patti started to run again. She stopped when she was close enough to see Jamie's misty breath and his face intent on counting.

"Seventeen, eighteen . . ." he was saying.

"Jamie, you have to come! Please come!"

He look up, surprised to see her tears. "What's wrong, Pats?" he asked.

"They're going to kill the little dog if we don't hurry," she sobbed.

"Where? What're you talking about?"

"A bunch of dogs in the gravel pit. Oh *please* come, Jamie," she begged.

Jamie hesitated a moment.

"I'll have to get a stick or something," he said. "And a flashlight."

Patti knelt in the snow and worked on her boots while Jamie ran back to the house. Her mitts were balled with snow. She tossed them impatiently aside, wiping her eyes first before she tackled the frozen laces. She was ready by the time the kitchen door slammed.

Stretching into the footprints she had made a few moments before, Patti led Jamie across the field. She could hear her own puffing and Jamie's harsh breathing behind her.

But that was all she could hear in the cold evening air. She suddenly stopped still beside the fence as she realized what that meant: there was no more yelping or howling from the gravel pit.

Jamie was looking at the fence, now lying useless in the snow, and he thought he knew what was bothering her.

"It's okay, Patti," he said. "We'll come back and fix it in the daylight. We don't need to tell Dad."

"No! It isn't that!" she said. "I can't hear the dogs any more."

In a moment she was through the mess of wire and post and running around the edge of the dark pit. She stopped once more to listen. But there were no sounds at all to guide her. Nothing to indicate where she should look.

"Where are they?" Jamie came panting up behind her, flashlight in one hand and his Boy Scout staff in the other.

Patti scanned the top of the dark hollow. She spotted, at last, the place where the gravel-pit road joined the main road.

"It must be a little farther around the edge," she said.

In a few minutes, they stopped beside a willow above the ledge where the little dog had crouched. In the light of the flashlight she could see that the snow had been trampled all around them and that a beaten track led over the edge.

"Down there." She pointed at the slippery path.

Jamie beamed his powerful light around the slope beneath them. But there were no dogs. In the depths of the gravel pit, nothing moved. Back and forth the light slid over the snow. At last, in a hollow below a small evergreen tree, it came to rest on a patch of something that stained the beaten snow. A speckled trail led from there down into the pit.

They stood and looked for a long moment. In the beam of the flashlight, it was more a dark grey than red, but Patti knew that it was blood.

Later that evening, Patti kneeled on her bed in the darkness, pulling the curtain back. The light from the kitchen window cast a golden square on the snow outside, and the others, Dad and Jamie and Mom, were hauling buckets of water. They tipped them carefully into the packed square of snow that lay inside the square of light. Tomorrow, it would be a skating rink.

They had eaten supper already, but Patti hadn't wanted any. After she and Jamie had walked home and peeled off their frozen snowsuits next to the stove, she realized that she didn't want to work on the rink tonight. Especially, she didn't want to sit at the bright kitchen table and listen to the chatter and excitement of the project. She wanted to get into her pyjamas and crawl under her two warm quilts, and try to forget the gravel pit.

In the quiet of her bedroom, she heard Jamie telling Mom and Dad the story of the dogs. After that, she heard the water running at the kitchen sink.

"Cold?" Mom had called.

"Yep," Dad called back. "We don't want it to melt the snow underneath."

Again and again the kitchen door banged, while bits of conversation drifted up to Patti's room.

She was feeling better now. It was nice to kneel in her dark room with a quilt around her shoulders and watch her family going back and forth, talking and laughing.

Jamie said something to Dad; suddenly, they both put their buckets down and Dad chased Jamie around and around the rink until they both fell in a shrieking heap in the snow. Patti smiled a little to herself in the dark.

Then she saw the first of the drifting snowflakes. Oh, oh, she thought. The others hadn't noticed yet; they were still bustling cheerfully back and forth. She and Jamie had crossed their fingers for no snow tonight—new snow, before the surface froze, would make their rink too rough, so they would have to haul more water tomorrow night.

Patti watched the swirl of the gathering flakes against the dark sky. Oh, well. She would help with the water tomorrow night. Tomorrow night she would feel like it. Right now, she couldn't help hoping it would just keep on snowing, so that maybe, by tomorrow morning, it would have covered all the blood in the gravel pit.

Cold Snap

IT WAS MAGIC IN THE LANE. The rain had knocked off all the snow from the trees; water drops, frozen into wavy bumps and icicles along every branch, shone like prisms in the bright sunshine.

Patti stepped carefully so she wouldn't fall again. The snow underfoot had looked shiny, but safe enough—until suddenly her feet shot out from under her. It was while she was lying there, sprawled on the cold ground, looking up at the bare sparkling trees and the blue sky, that she first noticed the rainbows on the branches.

Luckily her skates had flown free, landing in a harmless tangle up against the fence. She looked thoughtfully at the blades as she pulled them out of the hard-packed snow: they could have really hurt her if she had fallen on them. From now on she would carry them in her hand instead of around her neck.

"Go on, Jamie! Take it!"

She could still hear the boys on the rink beside the house. It was strange to think that just a few minutes before she had wanted so desperately to be part of that game. Now, in the silence of the lane, where the last of the snow was packed along the roadway and scattered in icy patches on the fields around her, she was glad she had decided to go off to the woods alone.

Dad had told them last night that today would probably be the last Saturday for skating. It might be the final cold snap—it was, after all, the middle of March. Jamie had phoned around and persuaded most of his friends to turn up this morning to play hockey. But Patti's friend Joan didn't have skates—they always took turns with Patti's skates when she came to play. And Ruth had gone to Florida with her family for the Easter holidays.

"Can I play hockey with you?" she had asked Jamie this morning at breakfast.

"Aw, Patti," said Jamie. He looked anxiously at Mom, who was busy at the sink with her back to them. Dad had already headed out to the barn.

"You told me I was getting good," Patti had argued. She spoke loudly enough to be sure Mom heard, but without much conviction. Even *she* knew that a "good" ten-year-old skater couldn't compete with the speed of Jamie's twelve- and thirteen-year-old friends.

"What about Patti having a corner of the ice for herself?" Mom had suggested without turning around. She was scrubbing the last bucket of carrots from the root cellar. "That's how you've solved the problem before, isn't it?"

"Okay," muttered Jamie. He stacked his dishes to carry to the sink. "It's just that there's a lot of guys coming. It's going to be crowded," he explained.

It sure *was* crowded. Funny, Patti thought—as she laced up her skates half-heartedly and watched ten boys whiz around on their small rink—they hadn't had so many kids turn up at the same time the whole winter. Her corner was a bit of an off-shoot from the main rink, created accidentally when they were carrying buckets of water to make the rink. Some of it had spilled, melting the soft snow underneath and creating a circular annex about four feet across. It was their "home" when they played tag.

Patti went around it a few times, stopping to watch the boys or wave at Mom in the kitchen window. She pulled her fingers out of the ends of her mitts and fisted them together against her coat to warm them up.

Then she remembered a sunny afternoon two days before, when she had gone down the back lane with Mr. Wallace to help him carry sugar syrup to the beehives. They had been surprised to notice how much the creek had flooded from all the rain and melting snow. The trees in the low land near the creek stood, as Mr. Wallace had observed, "up to their knees in water." Maybe in this last cold snap all that water had frozen solid. Would there be paths of ice winding in and out among the trees?

Yes. Patti could see them even now as she came to the end of the lane. Fingers of frozen creek pushed their way—who knew how far?—deep into the woods. The sun, still low in the south, shone through the dark branches of the wood lot, catching here and there on an expanse of ice and shooting fireworks into the crisp morning air.

She moved tentatively onto the stream. The ice held without so much as a crackle. She put her skates down and stepped out into the centre of a large patch, jumping up and down to test its strength. But the water was shallow everywhere, except perhaps in one part of the creek near the bridge. Here, it was frozen right down to the pebbles along the bottom.

Does the ice go all the way to our playhouse in the woods? Patti wondered. She stopped lacing up her skates for a moment to blow on her hands. Maybe it made a road now, right up to their door—that funny little gate door that she and Joan had woven last summer from willow shoots and propped upright in the gap between two tree trunks.

Hey, this would be a good time to build a stick wall around the whole house, now that the branches were bare.

But Joan would call it a barricade—she would make secret escape routes and mount cannons at every corner. And she would definitely want a bonfire.

But "no fires" was the rule. Patti had asked Mom and Dad again and again—every time Joan made a fuss about it—but they wouldn't change their minds.

It was silent as Patti cruised slowly along the slippery path, watching carefully for twigs and bumps in the ice that might catch her blades. She missed the birds of summertime. It was too quiet—the woods didn't seem like *her* woods. Her skates, sliding over the hard ice, crinkled like paper being folded. Their sound was muffled by the tall trees around her, leaning over, their frozen arms like bones, bare of leaves and snow. No sound at all came into the woods from the outside. Not even the shouts of Jamie and his friends up at the rink.

She should have phoned Joan. Though she probably wouldn't have been able to come out, anyway—she didn't seem to have as much time to play in the winter as she did in the summer.

As she glided deeper into the woods, even the morning sun had a hard time creeping between the thick maple trunks and the pine trees. It was dark. Should she go back now? Yet the frozen path led on and on, around this tree, then along the hollow, then back into a thicket. Patti pushed aside some fallen branches to clear the way to a spot where the trail suddenly joined a wider highway among the trees.

Crunch.

What was that?

Patti stopped, one skate poised on its toe and her mittened hands reaching out for an alder sapling.

Had she imagined it? No, there it was again. Crunch.

But it was more like a scraping sound this time. Where did it come from? The cows were in the barnyard today—so, what could it be?

Patti searched the darkness of the woods behind her while she listened intently, her misty breath spiralling up into the branches.

"Patti!"

It was Mom. Patti let out her breath slowly, suddenly aware of the pounding in her chest.

"Mom?" Her voice sounded far away, even to herself. She tried again.

"Hi, Mom! I'm in here!"

Patti followed her own skate marks around the trees, hurrying back out into the daylight. It was Mom all right, a bundled figure beside the little bridge, beaming and waving at her. She had red cheeks and sparkling eyes. Patti stopped to look at her curiously: she looked young today, not like anybody's mother at all.

Mom swung a pack to the ground and unhooked her skates from around her neck.

"May I come skating with you?" she called. "It looks as though you got the best of the skating bargain after all."

"Yeah!"

Patti was delighted. She couldn't remember the last time Mom had had time to play with her.

"Does the ice go far into the woods?" Mom asked as Patti scrunched to a flashy stop beside her, just the way Jamie had taught her.

"I don't know yet," said Patti. "I was just starting to find a path to our playhouse. I was just wishing . . ." She felt suddenly embarrassed, admitting this to Mom. "I was just wishing I had phoned Joan to come. It's too dark in there, by myself."

Mom pulled her laces tight.

"Y'know, Patti," she said thoughtfully, "I bet my skates will fit Joan by next winter—she's getting to be a big girl. We could put tissue in the toes or something, if we need to."

Mom stood up and put her skate against Patti's. "See— there's not *that* much difference, any more."

And it was true—Mom's skates were a lot scruffier looking, but only a size or two bigger.

"C'mon," said Mom. "Let's see how far into the woods we can make our road." In an instant her white coat had disappeared among the black trunks and the tangle of bare branches.

"What about the pack?" Patti called, but there was no answer.

Patti looked at it, abandoned in the snow. Lunch, I bet,

she thought. She shrugged, swung it over her own shoulders, and followed Mom among the dusky trees.

Now, where had she disappeared so quickly? Patti examined the tracks in the light dusting of snow over the ice, but she had made such a confusion of tracks herself, going both ways, that it was hard to tell which were Mom's. She checked each offshoot of the path—at least that way she could tell where Mom *hadn't* gone.

And then she came to the end of her own trail. Not a sign. How could Mom have just vanished? Patti's exasperation felt so familiar—wasn't this just *exactly* the sort of stupid thing that Joan would have done?

"Mom!" she called as she peered into the gloom. She noticed that a rising wind picked its way over the snow in puffs along the top of a small hill.

Thump! Patti gasped. A hard snowball hit her square in the middle of the pack.

"Gotcha!" came a gleeful shout from somewhere in the tangle of snags and windfalls to her right.

"Argh!" said Patti in disgust. She realized she had walked right into the trap. She would have had more sense than to do that with Joan.

Quickly, she slipped off the pack and dived behind a clump of poplar saplings. She saw the next missile just in time to duck as it crashed into the snow behind her. Aha! That one had come from behind the big pine tree close to the trail.

Patti pushed through the crust to find a handful of icy snow and packed it down into a hard ball. At the same time, she kept her eyes on the trunk of the pine. Suddenly she spotted a flash of white as it darted behind a closer clump of trees. She crawled behind a bush, then stood up to make three short leaps behind some wide black trunks. She hoped they were a good shield.

Mom's next snowball was way off its mark, she noted with satisfaction. It exploded yards away, against a rocky bluff. The enemy was just guessing now. Patti peered cautiously around a trunk and waited for Mom to give herself away. Meanwhile she stockpiled her own ammunition.

Sure enough, in a moment the white figure slipped from behind a tree and stuck her head above some bushes to search the woods near the spot her last snowball had landed. A perfect target. Patti got to her feet carefully, aimed and threw. Then she ducked quickly behind the trunk again to grab the next ball.

"Ouch!"

Patti giggled and peered around the tree to watch Mom laughing and brushing herself off. She wasn't taking the slightest care any more to keep hidden. She was so close.

Patti threw again. This time she missed, but took advantage of Mom's surprise to land another neat hit on the back of her legs.

"I give up! I give up!" Mom was laughing so hard, with her arms up around her head, that her skates slipped, tumbling her into a bank of snow. Patti grabbed the two balls she had left and scrunched through the snow on her skates towards her, stopping twice to throw them into the huddled and squealing Mom.

"You have to say 'mercy!', Mom," she said, reaching for another handful of snow. "If you don't say 'mercy,' I can't stop."

"Okay! Mercy!" It came muffled through Mom's arms as she peeked up at Patti.

When she sat up, still puffing, she grabbed Patti into a bear hug. "How did you get so good?" she asked.

Patti shrugged. What could she say?

"So . . . what about some lunch?" Mom asked suddenly, pushing Patti gently off her legs and struggling to her feet. She reached down to help Patti up. "Is your playhouse a good place to eat?"

"I don't know," said Patti doubtfully. "There's a table and some logs to sit on. But I haven't seen it all winter. It's probably pretty cold."

In fact, the wind had been getting up while she and Mom were having their snowball fight. Patti shivered as she brushed the snow off her pants.

"Let's find it," said Mom. She set off again along the frozen trail, stopping to pick up the pack. She turned to wait for Patti.

It was already darker—the sun must have gone behind a cloud. Patti was especially glad to have company with her now as she led the way among the trees, deeper and deeper into shadows. She tried to remember how the woods had looked in the green of summer, but it was hard to recognize anything.

It was the woven gate that gave away the playhouse. How funny it looked now, filling the space between two trees, while all around the rest of the house there were great empty places, usually filled by layers of leaves.

"Where should we build the fire?" asked Mom, as she slipped the pack off onto the frozen piece of plywood that was their table.

"A fire? Really?" said Patti.

"Only in winter, of course," said Mom. She looked at Patti for a moment, then grinned. She looked about Joan's age.

"Maybe you should always ask me first. Is that a bargain?"

"A bargain!" cried Patti.

She looked around to find the best place for a fireplace, pushing the pieces of wood that she and Joan used for furniture over to one side and clearing away some underbrush. Meanwhile, Mom had put some sandwiches on the table with two Thermoses. Then, out of the pack came a newspaper and four or five sticks of dry kindling. She had planned the fire from the beginning.

In a few moments it was crackling in the snow. What a difference it made—the warmth and the light and the comforting sound. They collected a pile of branches to burn, once the dry wood was well and truly going. Then Mom suggested that they make a windbreak by stacking up the logs that had served as furniture.

"It's warmer—but it doesn't look much like a house any more," Patti said, as she stood, hands on hips, to inspect the new arrangement.

"More like a fort," Mom agreed.

They spread some leafy fir branches on the ground, then put a small plastic tarp from the pack on top of them to sit on. Now they were dry, warm and sheltered. After they had eaten the sandwiches and the hot soup from one of the Thermoses, they cooked some bannock dough on two sticks they had peeled, and spread them with gobs of strawberry jam.

"Do you have any dishes?" Mom asked, looking around.

"Sure," said Patti. "The tea set that Gramma gave me. Remember? I took it back to the house for the winter, though."

"Very sensible," Mom said thoughtfully.

"You know," she said, after a few moments, "I packed away some of Gramma's old cooking pots and rolling pins and things. They're in a box in the basement. I'm sure you girls would look after them."

"Oh, yeah," said Patti enthusiastically. "But it's me who would play with them, you know. Not Joan."

Mom raised a questioning eyebrow at Patti.

"I guess she does that sort of stuff every day, at home," Patti explained. "When she can come and play, she wants to be . . . well, a pirate or something. Something different."

Mom nodded. She seemed to understand.

"But *I* like to play house," Patti said. "You know, cook and stuff. And Joan doesn't mind, as long as I do the work."

"That reminds me," said Mom suddenly, "I've got to head home right away—I've got a dentist appointment this afternoon. Are you going to stay?"

Patti leaned over and put a couple of branches on the fire. She was having fun.

"I think I'll just tidy things up a bit," she said. "Maybe see if I can put some sticks between the trees to make some proper walls. And I'll need a place for the pots and pans."

"Sounds good," said Mom, standing up and brushing snow off her pants. "But would you do something for me? Could you put the roast in the oven at four o'clock? It's getting dark by then, anyway, and you should be home."

"Of course," said Patti, surprised and pleased. Mom had never asked her to do something like that before.

"I'll write out the instructions in a note," said Mom. "I put some hot chocolate in the other Thermos—it'll warm you up in a little while. Br-r-r. I bet those boots we left back in the lane are frozen!"

Patti dragged open the gate so Mom could leave the house like a proper guest. She waved as the white coat and toque started off along the ice-road. Then she thought of something.

"Mom!" she called.

Her mother turned, rosy-cheeked in the grey light, to look back at Patti.

"Don't hang your skates around your neck when you walk up the lane," Patti shouted. "It's dangerous. You might fall and cut yourself on the blades."

Mom stood still for a moment. Then she waved her agreement and skated off among the trees.

Blizzard

IT WAS SNOWING HARDER NOW. Patti piled a large branch on her fire, then stood back to watch it crackle. Sometimes there were little explosions that lit her playhouse in the woods, sending sparks high up among the trees overhead, spotlighting the snowflakes.

She looked around with satisfaction. The wind blew stronger as it got darker out there among the trees, but that only made it cosier in here. Patti checked the watch Mom had strapped to her wrist. Only two o'clock. It must be the woods and the clouds that made it seem so dark. A fine dusting of snow had appeared on the table again, though she had brushed it off just a minute ago. She looked again at the trees above her, at the snowflakes that were beginning to multiply.

That gave her an idea. Why not use the tarp as a roof? Jamie had used it at Scout camp last summer, so it still had pieces of twine attached to all the grommets at the corners and along the sides. If she moved her "couch" of fir branches back a little bit, she could tie the tarp to the low-hanging branches right above it. She could even drag the table under her roof, so her pack and Thermos wouldn't get snowy.

It was more fun, Patti decided, to be doing this all alone. Friends were fun, and so was Jamie. Mom too. But right now, she could do this all by herself. She stood back, hands on her hips, to decide on the right place for the tarp. No arguments today. On the other hand, it would have helped to have someone taller. She would have to stand on a round of wood to stretch up high enough to reach the branches. But what about the skates she was wearing? Walking in them on the crusty snow wasn't so difficult— but teetering up there on a block of wood?

Patti looked at her skates in annoyance. Darn! How she wished she hadn't left her boots back at the end of the lane. If she walked around in her heavy socks, they would get snowy and wet.

Aha! Patti grinned as the solution came to her.

Rummaging through the knapsack, she found the plastic bag that had held the floury bannock mixture. She turned it inside out to shake out the flour dust that remained. Then she sat down to unlace her skate, grunting as she pulled it off. She fitted the bag over the sock. A rubber band would help, she thought, sticking her leg out to eye her new boot critically. But she didn't have any. Instead, she rolled her outside sock down as securely as possible over the top of the bag. Then she stumped around in a circle. It would do.

Next, she poked into all the corners of the knapsack for another plastic bag. Since Mom had packed the lunch, it meant that emergency nuts and raisins were certainly hidden somewhere. Sure enough, there they were in an outside pocket. Patti poured them loose back into the pocket of the pack and zipped it up. Then, with the two plastic bags over her feet, she began the tricky job of balancing on a round of wood, stretching on tiptoe to tie the tarp to the branches overhead.

It was colder up high—the wind whipped over the top of the little hill behind the playhouse, numbing Patti's fingers before she could get each knot tied. She hopped down and held her hands to the fire. Then she moved her round of wood once more and started tying the next length of string.

The way things were working out, the tarp was going to stretch beyond the windbreak behind the couch. What a waste of all that tarp. What if . . . Patti quickly untied her last knot and let the extra length of tarp drop. Then she jumped down and pulled it tightly to a tangle of sticks behind the couch, right against the windbreak. She tied both corners firmly, then she stood back. Perfect. Now she had a roof *and* a wall. And no wind at all in this snug little corner.

Her feet were getting cold. Patti took the plastic bags off and warmed her feet by the fire before she put her skates back on. Now, if she could just build some stick walls, so her gate didn't look so lonely . . .

Patti worked busily in spite of the awkwardness of walking in skates. She had to search quite far from the deep woods around the playhouse to find the tangles of brush that she needed. It was easier to walk, too, in the open where the snow was deep. But she never wandered out of sight of the fire—the winter woods looked so unfamiliar, and just imagine what Jamie would say if she was stupid enough to get lost on their own farm. Besides, she needed to stop and rest her feet often.

She pulled the clumps of brush apart, carrying the fat pieces back to feed the fire and using the long thin ones to weave into a wall. It was hard to get them long enough to bend around the tree trunks and bushes. But even a few good sticks made the playhouse seem more real. So she stopped working on the first section when it was still only up to her waist, and started on the one on the other side of the gate.

It was better already, she decided during one of her rest breaks by the fire. Now the gate looked useful, instead of standing there all alone and silly. Soon she would *have* to use it to get in and out of her house, instead of just walking through a gap between the bushes.

Patti stopped at last and leaned against a tree. She was having a hard time pulling a particularly big pile of sticks through one of those gaps: it kept snagging.

It was cold where the wind could blow. The snow was thicker, too. And it was gloomier. But in her playhouse, it was still bright and warm and cosy. Each addition to the wall kept out more of the dark. Wouldn't Mom be impressed with it now?

Mom. Patti suddenly dropped the boughs she was carrying and pushed her sleeve back to look at the watch. But it was too dark to see the numbers. She teetered on her skate blades along the hard ground between the trees and kneeled in the light of the fire. A quarter to four. And she had promised Mom she would put the roast in at four.

What a pity, Patti thought, as she stuffed the plastic bags and the Thermos into the knapsack. Just when things were going so well. She would leave the tarp up, anyway, and ask Mom about it. Maybe she would be allowed to keep it up for a few days longer. Maybe Joan could come and help her with the playhouse after school during the week. Especially if they could have a fire.

What about the fire? Should she put it out? Patti looked at it for a moment: in the last while, she had let it burn quite low. She would leave it, she decided. She tucked her extra pieces of firewood under a small fir tree beside her couch and carefully cleared the space right around the fire. That would do. It would be okay, she was sure. Especially on a day like today.

Slipping the pack on her back, she stepped out into the curtain of snow falling on the ice path, and began to skate slowly back the way she had come that morning. Her feet ached from the afternoon's work. It was worth it, though—she turned back twice to admire her playhouse, glowing among the trees.

But now, as the woods began to thin, she suddenly realized something awful: her tracks, and Mom's, had completely disappeared. At least three inches of snow had piled on top of the ice during the afternoon. There was no way, now, to tell the difference between the ice and the ground. No clear path back to the creek.

The wind blew harder: the swirling snow had turned into a blizzard so that she could hardly see beyond her own hand. Every moment or so her skates bumped smack into the ground; she had to feel around with her blades to find the ice path, again. Then she hit another rock. It was so slow. And what *was* the right direction, anyway?

Patti remembered all the little side paths she and Mom had passed on their way through the woods. Some of them were dead ends, and some went around in circles, and who knew where the others went? She was like one of the buttons in a game of snakes and ladders—any minute she could end up at the end of the lane, where she wanted to be . . . or right back where she started.

Suddenly Patti stood still. First she peered into the whirling dusk ahead of her. Then she turned and looked back at the small flicker of her fire that still reflected on the snowy branches above it. This was serious. How *did* she know this was the right way? She thought she had started off the way Mom had gone, but how could she be sure? And if she didn't know which direction to go, did that mean she was lost?

Patti listened to the wind. The new thought kept repeating: I'm lost! I'm lost! Sometimes, reading books, or listening to stories on the radio, Patti had wondered what it would feel like to be *really* lost. But she had never imagined it could happen right here, in her own woods.

What should she do? She opened her mouth to call "Mom!" then shut it again. Silly. Mom had been gone for hours. When had the weather gotten so bad? Why hadn't she paid attention? Should she *guess* which way to go? The farm wasn't so very big—sooner or later she ought to come to a fence that she could follow.

What she wanted now, more than anything, was to get home before anyone realized she was lost. Especially Jamie. If she could just manage to get that roast in the oven for Mom, surely everything would be all right again.

Patti peered through the gloom. *That* was probably the right way—the land seemed to slope down towards the creek. Then she could follow the creekbed . . . but *how* could she follow the creek? There were dozens of little creeks now, after all the flooding. And there was new snow to hide any clues.

Patti had already taken a few steps downhill, but now she stopped and turned back anxiously to look for signs of her fire. It had disappeared. Quickly she stumbled back the way she had come until, thank goodness! she could see the comforting glow again.

At that moment the blade of her right skate came down with a crunch on a hidden rock. Ouch! Slipping sideways, it wrenched her foot from under her so that she tumbled headlong into the snow. She sat up quickly and reached for her ankle—oww-w, it hurt! It was hard to see in the wind and driving snow, but Patti pulled a mitt off with her teeth and felt for the laces of her skate. The pain eased immediately as she undid the top and released the pressure. Gritting her teeth, she pushed at the heel until the skate gave way; gently, then, she slipped it off her foot and cradled her pulsing ankle in her hands.

In a few moments, her bare hand was numb. Patti shook the snow off her mitt and slipped it back on. She knew that she had to get back to the fire. Quickly. There was no sense any more in trying to get home.

"Sorry, Mom," she said to the wind howling in the trees overhead.

Pulling off her other skate, she shook her shoulders

until the pack slipped to the ground. Inside, she found the plastic bags to put over her socks. Then she pushed at the blades of her skates to make them fit in her pack. At last she could zip it up. And now it was time to stand.

Patti took a deep breath. With both mitts in the snow, she pushed herself up onto her good foot. She stood slowly, swaying, then balanced herself gently on her sore foot. With a cry, Patti fell into the snow again. Her ankle hurt worse than ever. Sobbing, she held her foot in both hands. What should she do? It was so cold, and she couldn't walk at all. Even a little bit.

When the pain had settled into a dull throb and Patti's crying stopped, she discovered that she knew exactly what she should do. It was very important to get back to her fire before it went out. It was dangerous to stay out here in the cold any longer. Funny, she thought, how you could listen all your life to Maynard's stories about blizzards on the farm, and Mom and Dad's warnings about what not to do, and still end up in such a dangerous situation. And take so long to realize it.

Stay where you are: that was rule number one. Find a shelter close by: number two. When Mom and Dad came looking for her, she should be at her playhouse. That would be the first place they would look. She would just have to crawl there. And she'd better do it fast, before she got any colder.

Wriggling the straps of the pack back over her shoulders, Patti eased herself onto her knees. She raised her sore foot awkwardly in the air as she crawled through the powdery snow. It throbbed whenever she moved, but it was bearable. She soon discovered that her hands and knees, which ached from the cold ground and from the weight of her body and her pack, hurt as much as her foot.

Patti decided not to even try to find the path back to the fire; instead, she set a straight line through the underbrush towards the distant glow. The wind was shrieking now, the snow driving sideways. Close to the ground, among the roots and stumps and snags, it was warmer and more sheltered than when she pulled herself up with the help of a small tree to peer through the blizzard and find the fire again. What a relief to see the glow still there. But although she kept on steadily, it never seemed to get any closer. Of course, it must be going out.

Time and again she had to turn aside and take the long way around a fallen tree. Then she had to pull herself upright and search for the flickering light, to be sure she was still going in the right direction.

And then, she lost it. The fire disappeared. Shivering as she clung to the trunk of a tree, she looked in every direction, straining upwards, crouching lower. It must be there. But there was nothing to see except snow and darkness. What could she do now?

It was the popping sound that saved her. That's what she told Dad and Jamie a little while later, when they stumbled through the blizzard into the shelter of her playhouse.

Patti heard them long before she saw them.

"Patti! Patti!"

But they couldn't hear her.

"I'm here!" she had shrieked into the wind until her voice was hoarse. Then she started yanking branches out of her wall to make the fire as bright as possible.

"Popping sound?" Jamie was puzzled. He had his hat and mitts off by then, and was holding his hands out to the blaze. The wind shrilled overhead. Dad was sitting on the fir branches under the tarp, holding Patti tightly on his lap.

"Yeah. The popping sound," said Patti. "I couldn't see anything familiar at all. I was sure I was completely lost. Then suddenly there was a loud pop, like there is sometimes in the wood stove when the fire is going out. That's when I realized I was right behind that," she said, pointing to the snug wall of wood rounds and tarp behind them.

"It was my own wall that blocked the little bit of light left in the fire."

"That's the way it is in a blizzard," said Dad, his voice deep and rumbly under Patti's ear.

"You think you're in some strange place, and all the while home is right around the corner. That's what makes it so dangerous."

"Well, Mom was right, wasn't she, Dad?" said Jamie.

"What do you mean?" asked Patti.

"When she called from town about five-thirty to say she would stay at Minnie's until the snow-plough came through, we told her you weren't home yet," said Dad.

"I was supposed to put the roast in at four," said Patti.

"She didn't care about that, you little goose," said Dad. "She was worried about *you*. I wanted to call out a search party right away, because I knew you could have gone off track anywhere between here and the house—especially after the storm got really bad."

"We thought you'd be so scared you would try to get home, even in the blizzard," explained Jamie.

"But your mom said 'no,'" Dad explained. "She told us to come straight to the playhouse before we called anyone—and to look out for your fire. She had a hunch this is where you'd be."

"We came along the lane fence, so we wouldn't get lost too," said Jamie, "and then we tied a rope to the bridge . . ."

". . . where we found your boots hanging over the railing," Dad added.

"Mom must have put them there," said Patti.

"Every time the rope ran out, we tied another one to it," Jamie explained. "That's how we got here. And that's how we'll find our way back to the house."

It was just like one of Maynard's stories, thought Patti.

"And if we don't get on our way soon," said Dad firmly, "Mom will send out a search party after *us*. Wouldn't that be embarrassing?"

"Oh, no!" exclaimed Jamie, jumping up and putting on his hat. "That would be awful."

"A search party isn't so awful if you're *really* lost," said Patti with conviction. She grinned up at Dad as she clutched his arm for support.

"That's what you guys are—and you're not awful at all."

Tree Blood

"It's like blood," said Patti. "Tree blood." She put her finger under the shiny spout, then licked the drop of sap. It tasted clear and cool, with just a hint of sweet. Like early spring.

"Don't be crazy!" Jamie shook his head in disgust. "How can a tree have blood?"

"It just makes me think of blood," insisted Patti. "Tapping maple trees is like taking some of their blood."

She stood back suddenly and looked up at the maple, its black branches reaching high, as delicate as lace against the late afternoon sky.

"I hope it doesn't hurt them," she said.

"Hey, do you want to do this or don't you?" Jamie was fed up now, his hands on his hips. "Just because Pete can't, it doesn't mean I can't get someone else to help."

"It's okay," said Patti. "I'll do it."

"Then we have to start tomorrow morning," said Jamie. "My teacher says the best time is right now. That means you'll have to be up early and ready to go with me. And you'll have to pull your own sleigh when we start collecting."

"I can do that," said Patti. "That's easy."

"And no more talk about blood."

Patti laughed.

"I mean it!"

Patti looked at her brother, surprised. She always counted on Jamie to put the worms on her hook when they went fishing. And he made fun of *her* when she went to visit a friend to get away from the farm on the days the chickens had to be butchered. Could he *really* be upset by a little tree blood?

"Okay," she said at last. "It was just an idea."

Later, at the supper table, Dad looked a little doubtful about their project

"There's nothing really wrong with the plan," he said, "except I don't think there are enough maple trees down in the bush—not enough to make all your effort worthwhile. You need so much sap to boil down into a small amount of maple syrup. Do you know how much it takes?"

"Oh, yeah," Jamie nodded eagerly. "Mr. Davies told us all about it."

"What do you want the syrup for?"

"Well, some for my science project," explained Jamie. "With pictures and diagrams and a diary of everything I do.

"But . . . ." He hesitated a moment. "I thought I'd like to see if I could make enough to sell. I want to make some money—so I don't have to ask you for stuff. Like a new hockey stick. And I'll need new skates in the fall."

"I suppose . . . well, there doesn't seem to be any money for *us* to pay out for this venture," said Mom, chin in hand. She was looking at Jamie thoughtfully.

"You could use the summer kitchen stove—maybe you could split enough wood to replace what you use. There's my big canning pot for the boiling. And jars—I've collected a lot more than I need."

"I bought twenty-five spouts today," said Jamie. "I had some Christmas money left."

"Twenty-five! Do you really think you can find that many trees?" Dad looked sceptical.

"There are five just along the road, you know. I've tapped them already."

"Well . . . I could phone our neighbour tonight, I suppose," suggested Dad, "to see if they have any objection to you tapping the maple trees in their part of the wood lot down by the river. That way, you can make the most of the long walk there and back. I'm sure a jar of maple syrup would be plenty of payment."

"Thanks!" Jamie was beaming.

"What about me?" Patti asked her brother.

"What do you mean?"

"Well, if I help you, do I get some of the money?"

Jamie looked disconcerted.

"I . . . I suppose so," he said.

"Now *that's* something you two need to decide before you even start," said Dad. "We don't want any labour disputes at the supper table."

Patti found herself mulling over their agreement as she struggled awake before daylight next morning. It was Saturday, and Dad had pounded on her door, as promised, on his way out to the barn. She would get one-third of whatever they made, after Jamie paid himself for expenses. It seemed fair . . . the whole thing was Jamie's idea, after all, and he was bigger and stronger and would probably do a lot more of the work.

But Jamie's money-making scheme had started her thinking. She had some money left from Christmas too. Just how much *could* they make with the maple syrup? If they worked really hard today, could they find even more than twenty-five trees? *She* could buy some more spouts this time. The thing was, maybe some day she would have a chance to have a pony . . . and, well, if she had saved enough by then, it might make all the difference. Her thoughts buzzed with possibilities as she pulled on her snow pants and tied her boots.

"We'll do the first two trees together, so I can show you how," said Jamie as they walked along the stubbled field in the pale wintry light. The road led to the big wood lot at the bottom of their farm. Patti didn't know this wood very well—it was farther from the house, bigger and darker, not as friendly as the one on the other side of the farm where she had built her playhouse. But *her* wood, with its cedar trees, birches and poplars, was too swampy for sugar maples.

"See those two big ones at the edge of the wood? I'll show you how to tell a sugar from a silver or red maple. It's the bark—the way the ridges curl outwards. Mr. Davies showed us."

Jamie's voice was muffled by his grey scarf and his breath escaped through the gaps into puffs of condensation. The sky was clear—the sun would shine warmly later in the day, but right now, Patti was glad she had gone back to the house to get a second pair of mitts. Their sleighs slipped smoothly over the frozen ground. Strapped on top of each sleigh was a five-gallon bucket filled with clean juice tins, to which they had fastened home-made wire handles. Also in the bucket were the metal spouts, a brace and bit, and a hammer.

"It's simple, see?" said Jamie, a few minutes later, as his hand whirred around on the brace and bit, drilling through the gnarled bark and dropping white sawdust down the side of the tree.

"Watch now, Patti—as soon as the sawdust comes out damp. See? That means we've reached the layer where the sap comes up."

He pulled out the bit and reached for the first spout. In a moment he had hammered it into the hole and hung a juice tin on its hook.

"Now it's your turn," he said, pulling his sleigh to the neighbouring tree.

"See the bark?"

Yes, Patti could see now what made a sugar maple different from the other maples. But the brace and bit was awkward in her mittened hands, and the spout went in crooked the first time. She had to pull it out, take her mitts off and try again.

"You'll do better next time," said Jamie. "But now I've gotta go, so I can scout the deeper part of the wood and go over the fence into the neighbours'. We've got to hurry—Mr. Davies says we'll be lucky to have a week this year before the spring is too far along."

"What happens if the spring gets too far along?" asked Patti.

"I guess the leaves come out and the sap stops flowing," Jamie answered. "Mr. Davies says it gets too thick and doesn't taste very nice before it stops."

"But won't I get lost in these woods by myself?" asked

Patti, looking ahead to where the logging road curled away and disappeared among the trees.

"No," said Jamie, "because you'll do the maples you can see from the road. Also, you're going to keep track of me with this."

He pulled off his mitt and reached into his pocket for his Scout whistle. He handed it to Patti.

"I borrowed Pete's so I could have one too. Every ten minutes or so, I'll blow and you'll answer. We have to work fast. Especially since Mom says we *have* to be home for lunch."

Jamie made a face and Patti nodded sympathetically. But her feet were cold already, and she was glad Mom had decided on that rule.

"Be reasonable," Mom had argued with Jamie at breakfast. "If it takes you more time than that to tap the trees, you won't be able to collect the sap from them after school, anyway. Besides, you have your Saturday chores to do."

An hour later, Patti's hands, minus her mitts, were freezing even more than her feet, and she was thinking already about the warm living room that she would dust and vacuum that afternoon; the eggs that she would clean and pack, cuddled up close to the kitchen stove.

It was hushed beneath the big trees—the poplar and cedar in the lower spots, the birch and maple on the rises—as if they were already awake after a long sleep and just waiting for a sign. Did they see her down here in her white coat and red scarf? Her hands, stiff and blue, turned the brace and bit as she watched the sawdust until it became wet with sap. Tree blood.

Each time she hung a juice tin on the hook beneath a spout, she stopped for a minute, shoving her cold fists into her pocket, and looked up at the bare branches of the tree she had just tapped. She didn't exactly *say* thank you, but that's what she felt. She realized that after this morning's work, she would never feel like a stranger in these woods again.

I'm in a hurry, she kept reminding herself.

Soon she had done seven trees all by herself, each one appearing like a surprise before she had to really look. Now, over on a slight rise, was yet another promising cluster of three or four, yet she hadn't even reached the point where the road looped back to join itself. This was much better than they thought it would be, she thought with satisfaction. Even pulling Jamie's sleigh along with hers was no problem; in fact, soon she would have to start using his tins and spouts. Luckily he had carried only four sets with him into the bush.

Where was Jamie? She expected him to come crashing through the undergrowth any minute now to get more tins, because she hadn't heard his whistle for a while.

Could he have forgotten about the signal? she began to wonder. Where was he, anyway?

Suddenly two bright blasts pierced the cold morning air. Patti wiggled her numb fingers into her jacket pocket for her own whistle so she could reply. But there was no time for her to put the whistle to her mouth. Jamie's shrill signals started once more, but this time they didn't stop: they went on and on while Patti stood in amazement.

And then she understood: Jamie's in trouble. He wants me to come.

Patti dropped both rope handles. She hesitated for a moment at the edge of the road, then plunged into the wood towards the commotion. The snow, hard-packed and icy along the exposed roadway, was still piled in drifts here and there among the trees. Patti stopped, puffing, to put her mitts back on. Then off she charged again, running up the banks where they were crusty enough to hold her, and ploughing through them when they turned out to be soft.

Deep into the woods she ran towards the frantic whistle blasts, through brushwood, under leaning trees, over fallen trunks, stopping every few minutes to listen intently. Soon they became slower, farther apart. Her whistle was still in her hand. She blew it twice into the silence, then listened. This time two ordinary blasts answered her. He knew she was coming. Once again she turned her attention to the obstacles ahead of her. Would she ever make it through the piles of snow and tangled underbrush?

It was Jamie's light grey scarf that caught her attention—in the gloom under the trees, it gleamed against his navy snowsuit and hat. And it was much higher up than she expected. Jamie lay at a peculiar angle along

the top of the fence near the point where it turned a corner, the old posts leaning inwards and holding him
strangely suspended above the snow. Beneath him, on a
grey, crusted drift, was a large spatter of blood.

"Jamie!" Patti called.

There was no answer.

She ran as hard as she could through the debris of
branches and old snow. Breathing hard, she came close to
him cautiously at first. She didn't speak or reach out to
touch him. She needed to figure out why it was that he lay
like this, as helpless as a broken branch, along the top of
the fence. One foot supported him on a fence strut, and
some of the barbed wire, which was strung along the top
of all their perimeter fences, had tangled itself somehow in
his snowsuit. In a hole in the snow, beside the splashes of
blood, lay Pete's whistle.

"Jamie?"

He lifted his head briefly to acknowledge her, then laid
it back on the mittened hand clutching a clump of fence
wire.

"You'll need my Scout knife," he said, "to cut the
barbed wire. In my pants pocket. The one facing you."

His voice was quiet and calm.

Relieved, Patti looked at his pocket, which was right in
front of her, almost at eye level.

"But . . . but Jamie," she said, "I *can't* cut that heavy wire
with your knife."

"Then get Dad," he said, his voice muffled against his mitt.

She turned, hesitated, then turned back to Jamie. The hour it would take to get back here with Dad would be much too long.

She reached out to touch the pocket.

"Careful," said Jamie. "*Careful!*"

Pulling her hand back, Patti looked more closely at the tangle of cloth and fence. She could see, now, how the barbed wire emerged from the inside of Jamie's leg, through the torn snow pants. She understood why there was blood still dripping onto the snow underneath.

Gently, she eased her hand into the slippery material of the pocket. Slowly, slowly she worked her fingers further in. She could feel Jamie shaking.

There it was—the knife. The thin leather she could feel was the lanyard. She caught it between her fingers and pulled until it slipped free of Jamie's pocket.

It wasn't until she had opened the blade that she knew what she was going to do. Starting with the pocket opening, she began to cut through the snow pants on the side facing her. Around she went, almost to the back; then to the front, above the point where wire and pants were hopelessly tangled. The tough cotton outer layer ripped easily before the sharp blade. Next came the insulation, grey and matted, which practically pulled away in her fingers. Then the inside layer of cloth. Then Jamie's grey sweat pants. These were close to his skin in some places—she had to be careful, lifting it away, then inserting the point of the knife.

Jamie wasn't shaking now—he lay quietly and waited for her to finish.

She stood back and looked at the mess the wire had made. Prodding tentatively at the ripped blue material, she discovered that the prongs of barbed wire were wrapped in the cloth—which meant they weren't in Jamie's leg any longer. So . . . if she continued cutting the torn part away, she could probably free his leg, leaving behind the pieces of his pants that were hooked by the fence.

Concentrating, careful not to push the sharp fence up against Jamie, she cut a circle around the layers of torn cloth and blood, then gently, ever so gently, she eased the bunched material away from the leg.

"Jamie!" she cried suddenly. "It's bleeding again. Fast!"

"You'll need a tourniquet." Jamie had lifted his head again. "You've got to tie something around my leg above the bleeding."

Her red scarf. Patti looped it between Jamie's leg and the fence. Blood dripped quickly into the snow. She twisted the scarf around itself and pulled it tight. Immediately the bleeding slowed.

"Tighter," said Jamie, his face down against his mitt again. "It has to be tighter than that."

Once again, Patti pulled the two ends of the scarf, afraid to hurt Jamie, but also afraid the bleeding wouldn't stop. She wrapped the longest end around his leg once more, then tied a knot. The bleeding was back to just a drip now and then.

What should she do now?

"Jamie," she said. "You're going to have to put your weight on that leg, so you can lift your other leg over the fence."

"I don't know if I can," said Jamie. He sounded small and very frightened.

"You have to," insisted Patti.

"Look," she said, "I'll stand right here and hold the wire away from your leg, and you can lean against me. Come on, Jamie!"

Jamie reached carefully with both hands to grab the broken strut underneath him. Then, with a grunt, he pushed his shoulders up and, bracing his hurt leg against one of the posts, he lifted his other leg up and over.

"Uggh!" he groaned as he fell against Patti. A second later they were both sprawled in the snow.

The bleeding! In an instant Patti was up and bending over Jamie. His face was a strange yellowy-grey, and his torn leg, bare under the flapping snow pants, oozed blood. But it only oozed. It would be okay for a while longer. He looked up at her, but he didn't say anything.

Patti stood undecided for a moment. Then she took off her snowsuit jacket and wrapped it carefully around Jamie's upper legs.

She eased his toque down carefully over his ears.

"I can't pull your sleigh over all the branches and stuff to haul you back home, so I'm going to get Dad," she said. "Don't move, or you might start the bleeding again."

She turned to run, hesitated, then said to him, "It might take a long time, Jamie—it's a long way. I'll go as fast as I can."

Jamie nodded and closed his eyes.

But it didn't take very long at all. Patti had barely stumbled out of the deep woods, when she saw Dad cross the main road at the top of the hill and begin his long-legged run down towards her.

"When I got back from town," he explained later, "I just got the notion, somehow, to stop at the end of the drive and get out of the truck to see if I could see you two on your way home yet. And there was my crazy girl," he said, looking at Patti, "tearing along in the winter sunshine without her jacket.

"You used to do the same thing when you were about two, you know," he said. Patti and Jamie laughed.

The house was warm, and Mom had just brought in a tray of hot chocolate. Jamie sat in Dad's arm chair, a pair of crutches leaning up against the foot stool. His leg would be fine, the doctor said, but he mustn't put weight on it until the stitches came out in a week or ten days. Patti would bring his schoolwork home with her every day so he didn't get behind.

"But I can still look after the stove in the summer kitchen while we boil the sap," he said. "And wash the jars. That is . . . " He hesitated as he looked questioningly at Patti.

"Do you want to keep up with the syrup?"

Was he *asking* her, instead of telling her?

Jamie misunderstood her silence.

"*You'd* get the two-thirds share of the money, you know," he said. "Since you'd be doing most of the work."

Patti grinned at him, her face flushed from the hot chocolate.

"Of course I'll do it!" she said happily.

Something new and very nice had just happened: Jamie seemed to be talking to her as if she were Pete or one of his other friends. Not just his little sister.

Is There Always a Better Way?

PATTI LUNGED AT JAMIE AND CAUGHT HIM by surprise. He staggered backwards, fell over his gym bag and soccer boots and landed with a thump on the floor. She laughed at his open mouth.

"Gotcha that time!"

In a second Jamie had hurled himself across the space between them, grabbed Patti's bare legs and flipped her backwards. Her head whacked the floor with a crack that made her teeth ache.

"*What* is going on here!" Mom stood in the doorway. Hands on hips she looked first at Jamie, still lying on his stomach on a pile of pyjamas and T-shirts and shoes. Then at Patti, who pulled at the skirt of her Guide uniform and rubbed the back of her head.

"Jamie," Mom said at last, "I want this room tidy and you downstairs in five minutes. Patti, I've made the sandwiches. I want you to pack them in the bags—apples for everybody and two cookies. Then you can run out with Dad's bag and Thermos and put them in the pickup—he'll be finished in the barn in a couple of minutes. After that, I want to talk to you both before the school bus comes."

"Wu-hoo," said Jamie when she was gone. "Guess we're in for a lecture. You okay, Pats?"

"Yeh," said Patti. "It was just an accident. I don't see why she's so mad."

"It's like this, kids" said Mom a few minutes later. She paused for a long moment, stared out the window and took another gulp of coffee. Patti and Jamie looked at each other as the kitchen clock ticked into the silence.

"Well," said Mom, at last, "there are two things, really. No, three. One is that Jamie has been told before that he mustn't fight with girls. You're twelve now, Jamie. You're getting too big for this sort of stuff—you could hurt someone. You simply must not fight with girls. Do you understand?"

"But . . ." said Jamie.

"But what?" said Mom.

"Well . . . how is Patti going to learn *how*, if we aren't allowed to fight?"

"Patti doesn't *need* to learn how to fight," said Mom. "And that leads me to number two. You, young lady," she said, turning to Patti, "are going to have to learn to settle your differences without getting into scuffles. Especially with people bigger than yourself."

"It wasn't a real fight, Mom," Patti explained. "It was just fooling around."

"Well that's good, anyway," said Mom. "But number three is what I want you both to think about and remember: fighting never solves problems—it only makes more. There's always a better way."

Patti loved Guides and Brownies most of the time, but today wasn't quite so much fun. It was the new girl, Vanessa, who made things uncomfortable. Patti didn't like Vanessa very much, because even though she was new, she certainly wasn't shy about telling people what she thought. Her father was in the Air Force, so she had gone to a lot of schools and joined Guide groups that were much more exciting than the one here in this little town. And they weren't so small they had to have their meetings with little Brownies. Anyway, that's what she told everybody.

Today, Vanessa kept talking loudly while Brown Owl explained the day's project, and she pushed as they stood in line to get their craft supplies.

They were making dried-flower pictures for Mother's

Day. Brown Owl had taken blue pansies and yellow buttercups and little white daisies out of her flower press and put them into separate boxes.

"Be sure you just take two or three of each," she said, "so there are enough to go around. There are lots of green leaves over here to fill out your pictures."

Patti wanted to make her picture different from everybody else's. What about a border of leaves with flowers in the centre? She cocked her head to study the effect. Suddenly Deirdre jostled her elbow, and she turned impatiently to look.

"Patti," the little Brownie said softly, and Patti could see tears glistening on long black eyelashes.

Deirdre was in Grade One. She lived two farms beyond Patti's, and it was Patti's job, on Guides and Brownies days, when they stayed in town and missed the bus, to walk Deirdre home. She was a nice kid, really. Patti often thought she would like a little sister like Deirdre.

"Vanessa took my daisies," said Deirdre.

"She can't do that!" Patti was indignant. She followed Deirdre along a line of chattering girls to the end of the trestle table.

Vanessa seemed to be having a wonderful time. She had brushed a great stack of flowers and leaves to the edge of her cardboard and was busy squeezing a spirally bead of glue all over it.

Patti hesitated.

"You're not allowed to have that many flowers," she said politely.

She was suddenly uncertain—maybe Vanessa just hadn't understood Brown Owl. But the new girl didn't even look up from her loops of glue.

"I need more than you guys," she announced airily. "My picture is very complicated."

At that moment Brown Owl appeared behind them.

"Goodness," she said. "You've got a lot of flowers there for one person, Vanessa." She looked around at the other girls.

"Who doesn't have all her flowers yet?"

"Vanessa took my daisies," piped up Deirdre.

"But you see," explained Vanessa, "I'm making a whole garden for my picture—I have to have more than just *nine* flowers, don't I?" She was almost as tall as Brown Owl, and she waved the glue bottle around as she talked.

Brown Owl laughed and put her hand briefly on Vanessa's shoulder.

"You'll have to have a leafy garden, I guess, Vanessa," she said. "We've got piles of leaves in the box. I'll pass out your extra flowers to the girls who don't have them."

Vanessa shot Patti an angry glance.

"Thanks," she hissed, as Brown Owl moved out of ear shot. "You just ruined everything!"

But Patti had had enough of Vanessa. She went back to her Mother's Day card and tried to ignore the loud voice that went on and on above the general hubbub.

It wasn't over yet, though. Patti bounced down the old wooden steps of the hall after Guides and Brownies had been dismissed, with her pack on her back and her flower card waving in her hand. The spring sun was still warm at five o'clock, and a robin sang among the bright green leaves and maple clusters that overhung the entrance path.

Deirdre waited for her as usual by the road. Beside her stood Vanessa. She poked every now and then at Deirdre's picture, which the little girl held first over her head, then behind her back. She looked relieved to see Patti coming.

"I just want to *see* it," Patti heard Vanessa say. "I'm not going to *do* anything to it."

"Let's go, Deirdre," said Patti and started off along the dusty margin of the road. She walked quickly, so that by the time they had turned the bend and were out of town, her small friend puffed at her heels.

"Patti," Deirdre said, "look."

Patti swung around to see the new girl, a triumphant grin on her face, striding along just a few steps behind them.

"What's your hurry?" Vanessa jeered.

"Look," answered Patti, "just leave us alone. We want to go home."

"Yah . . . well, maybe I'm just going home, too," said Vanessa. "I can walk wherever I want." And she pushed between the two girls, jostling Patti and causing Deirdre to stumble for a moment.

"Watch it, eh!" said Patti. Her voice sounded gruff and her stomach flip-flopped. She was suddenly afraid. Up close, Vanessa seemed a lot bigger than she had in the Guide hall.

"Or what?" jeered Vanessa. "What can you and the little sissy here do about it?" She gave Deirdre another shove that knocked her into the roadway. Her picture flew, face down, on to the gravel margin.

Instantly, Patti's fear was gone. She felt a flush in her face and the tight clench of her fists, and she spoke through gritted teeth.

"Get away from us, if you don't want a fight!" She glared at Vanessa, then turned her back to help Deirdre get up and adjust her pack. She picked up the fallen picture and brushed it off. Her heart was pounding and she struggled to get her breath. But Vanessa was already at Deirdre again. The little girl was crying now as Vanessa gave her little pushes backwards and taunted.

"A crybaby sissy! Why don't you go and tell Mummy!"

Patti put the two pictures down carefully on the side of the road, slipped her pack off and set it on them gently so the wind wouldn't catch them. Then she flew at Vanessa, pushing with all her strength. Surprised, the bigger girl staggered to the edge of the ditch. When she regained her footing, she swiftly dropped her bookbag and rushed at Patti. But Patti was ready. Fists up, she watched Vanessa circle. Slap. A hand hit the side of Patti's head. Hard. Her ear stinging, she waited as Vanessa moved away and circled again. Patti jogged on the spot, arms raised and ready, just as Jamie had taught her.

Once more long arms reached out over Patti's fists and landed. Two punches this time. Then another. And another. But Vanessa had both arms busy now, and Patti knew this was the opening she had been waiting for. Fiercely she moved in under them, head down. Both hands jabbed at Vanessa's waist and chest, and she pushed with all her might. Vanessa took a step back, then two. She tripped over her pack and fell into the ditch. Patti was on top of her at once. Something noisy pounded in her head and she was ready for more.

Vanessa, however, was finished with the fight. Long, brown hair straggled into the grass; a scratch from a scrub branch bled into one eye. She looked small and helpless as Patti straddled her, a hand pinning each arm. Was she going to cry?

"Have you had enough?" Patti had trouble talking as she gasped for air.

Vanessa gave a slight nod. She looked away from Patti's face, so close to her own. Patti got up, brushed her bruised legs and rumpled Guide dress. She watched Vanessa until she sat up, then she turned to scramble up the bank of the ditch. Soon she and Deirdre were jogging down the hill towards the crossroads, on their way home.

Patti walked up the back steps and waited for a few moments with her hand on the doorknob. There was a chill to the air, although the sun was still shining. Her head ached, and she felt strangely sad.

Yet she had been feeling good just a short while ago, as she walked Deirdre to the path that cut across the field from her mailbox to her house. The two girls, once they had stopped running and could talk again, had laughed and giggled and joked about everything they saw along the way. They spotted the neighbour's golden Labrador as he sneaked away from home again. He was looking over his shoulder towards his house, so he didn't see Patti and Deirdre until he almost bumped into them. The expression on his face made them laugh until they hurt.

Then Patti gasped, "I have a stitch in my side."

Deirdre looked so surprised at the idea of a *stitch* in Patti's side that they started to laugh again. Then one of the kids from school drove past in a car and saw them stooped over, holding their sides. Her face at the rearview window, open-mouthed with amazement, set the girls off into hysterics again. After that, they told jokes because they wanted to laugh some more—old jokes that seemed funnier today than they had ever seemed before. But they didn't talk about Vanessa.

It was different for Patti now, though, as she stood with her hand on the doorknob. She remembered Mom's talk just that morning.

"Fighting never solves problems," she had said. "It only makes more."

Mom must be right, Patti thought. It was definitely a problem to feel as miserable as she did right then. But what else could she have done? She didn't know.

The kitchen was warm with the evening sunshine and the wood stove. Dad was slicing bread. He looked up as Patti came in.

"I was starting to wonder about you, Patti," he said.

And then he looked again. Patti glanced down at her grass-streaked Guide dress, her dirty legs.

"What on earth," said Dad as he put down his bread-knife and came to kneel in front of her. He pushed untidy hair away from her face.

"That's a nasty bruise on your cheek," he said softly. He looked so hard at Patti that somehow she couldn't stop the tears.

Dad gave her a long hug, then he said, "Come and sit down and have a glass of milk, Pats, and tell me about this."

She began with her scuffle with Jamie that morning, and Mom's rule about fighting. Dad nodded in agreement. Then she told him about Vanessa at Guides. He rubbed his chin and looked thoughtful when she described their walk home, and Vanessa pushing little Deirdre down. And then there was the fight. Patti faltered a little when she came to that part, and she began to cry again.

Dad waited for her to finish her story, and then he reached into his pocket and handed her a Kleenex. He said, "Why are you crying, Patti?"

She thought about it for a moment.

"I feel sad," she said. "I don't like that kind of fighting, I guess. I didn't feel sad while I was *doing* it—I was just so mad. And I didn't feel sad after, when I walked Deirdre home. I felt like I had done a good job."

Dad nodded encouragingly.

"It's . . . well, I keep thinking about Vanessa's face when she was lying in the ditch. She didn't seem very scary then. She just seemed like a little girl—like me. And even though she's lived in nicer places, she doesn't have any friends here."

"Do you think fighting solved her problem?"

Patti shook her head.

"Do you think it solved yours and Deirdre's problem with her? Will she pick on you again?"

"Maybe," said Patti. "Maybe not."

"Patti, do you think you could have done anything else this afternoon, when you walked Deirdre home?"

Patti shook her head slowly.

"Then I'm sure you did the right thing. And maybe you've reminded us—Mom and me—that fighting is sometimes more complicated than we would like it to be." Dad raised his eyebrow in a question.

"Where *is* Mom?" Patti asked suddenly, looking around the kitchen.

"She had to work late," said Dad. "But she'll be home by the time the casserole is hot. What *did* you learn today, Patti? Tell me."

"Well, let's see." Patti rested her chin in her hand and looked at her dad.

"Fighting doesn't really solve problems," she said thoughtfully. "That's just like Mom said. But there isn't *always* a choice about it—sometimes you just have to do it, even if it makes you feel sad."

Jamie pushed through the swinging kitchen door at that moment. He stopped when he saw Patti.

"Holy moley!" he said. "Look at that shiner! What've you been doin', Pats? Are you in trouble, or what."

"She's on her way upstairs to get clean for supper," said Dad. "And you, young man, have got just enough time to get the table set for dinner."

Little Guy

PATTI WAS IN THE BARN when Dad came home from work. Some old scraps of lumber were scattered around her and she was yanking at a bent nail at the end of one of them.

"Busy?"

"Ugh! I *hate* having to use old nails," she said, throwing down the hammer to grab pliers.

"Me too," said Dad.

He stood in the June sunlight just outside the door, watching Patti worry at the nail.

"What are you building?"

"A pen for Chicky," she answered. "So she can have her

own place at night, but be out in the barnyard during the day."

"She won't go in with the other hens, eh?" asked Dad.

"Chicky doesn't think she's a chicken," explained Patti. "She doesn't know how to push her way to the feed trough or the watering can. She just sulks and waits for me to come and pick her up! Soon she'll stop laying eggs."

"A separate pen's a good idea," said Dad. "I'll help you with it tomorrow.

"Patti . . ."

Dad seemed to be having a hard time saying something. Patti scrambled to her feet and ran out to join him in the sunshine.

"What's up?" she asked. It was Friday evening. Maybe something interesting was going to happen on the weekend.

"Your eleventh birthday is three weeks away . . ." said Dad.

Patti looked up at him, eyes shining. This was *definitely* interesting.

"Birthday presents are supposed to be surprises . . ." Dad was having real trouble finishing his thoughts. Patti looked at him curiously.

"C'mon inside, Patti," he said at last. "We need to discuss something with Mom."

Mom was making dinner. She looked up at Dad, saw Patti right behind him, and suddenly an 'aha!' look crossed her face.

She set down her chopping knife and put the kettle on for tea. She placed the cookie jar on the table.

A family conference—Dad and Mom had probably been planning something. But Jamie was still in town at his baseball game. It must be just about me, she thought, pulling out a chair. Excitement tingled in her stomach.

"First," said Dad, "I'd better spill the beans, and tell you that we've been keeping our ears open for a pony for you. For months."

Patti gasped. She had no idea.

"The trouble is," Mom put in quickly, "we just don't have the money for a pony—to buy it, feed it, pay for vet bills, buy the saddle and all the rest."

Oh. Patti knew this already. The tingle in her middle turned to something heavy.

"So . . . we have a proposal for you," said Dad. He stopped to gather his thoughts.

A proposal? For a birthday present?

"It's like this," he said finally. "What we are going to suggest is such a big commitment for you—and it might not be what you really want. It needs to be thought about and discussed in every little detail.

"This is a grown-up type of decision, Patti," he said, his forehead furrowed with concern.

"What *is* it?" Patti asked.

"Well," said Dad, "Mr. Cameron, at the mill, has a friend who lives about fifty miles from here. A Doug Anderson.

His teenage daughter has a horse—a small quarterhorse, almost a pony. She learned to ride on him. But she has just got a big new horse—a thoroughbred."

Dad stopped here to drink some tea and reach for a cookie.

Patti could hardly sit on her chair. Did the little horse have something to do with her?

"What this horse can't teach a new rider, Doug says, just isn't worth knowing. He's amazing with kids. But in the past couple of months the poor fellow's developed a foot inflammation. A kind of tendonitis, I think. He's seventeen years old—not really old for a horse, but the vet thinks he may never be cured. If that happens, he would never be able to enter horse shows, never jump again."

Oh.

Patti's racing mind suddenly flip-flopped and stuck on that last idea. No horse shows. No jumping.

Dad watched Patti for a moment, then looked up to meet Mom's eye.

"On the other hand," he went on, "given time and good care, he *might* get better. He also might improve for a while and then get lame again. No one really knows."

"So, they need someone to look after the horse?" Patti thought she was beginning to understand.

"It's not as simple as that," Mom said. She sighed.

"They *do* want someone to look after him," she

explained. "And they're very happy about you and our farm. They've already been here to talk to us. Doug and his daughter Lynne."

"Here?" Things were going so fast. "When?"

"Last Saturday, when you were at Ruth's," Mom answered.

"They're also pleased that you will be turning eleven—because that was her age when Lynne got Little Guy."

"That's his name? Little Guy?"

"Yes, that's his name."

Mom was fidgeting with the tea cosy.

"The point is, Patti," she said, "the Andersons would love to have you look after Little Guy—as long as you understand and agree to all their conditions."

"Conditions?"

"There are quite a few. I wrote them down."

Mom pushed a folded paper across to Dad.

"First, is their side of the agreement, if there is one," he explained. "They would bring all his tack and equipment with him—that means his saddle and bridle and blanket and so on."

Patti had a good idea how expensive those could be.

"Second, they would pay for the vet and the medicine and the blacksmith, if he ever has his shoes put back on."

"That's good, isn't it?" said Patti.

"They would also pay for his grain, if we supplied the hay."

"Now for *your* side of it," Dad went on. "And it could be very hard. So think about it carefully."

Patti swallowed.

"They would let you have Little Guy here for a year. But the horse would continue to belong to the Andersons. That means that all decisions about his future would be up to them—whether he would be sold to someone who could afford him, or put out to pasture."

Patti nodded. She understood so far.

"You would have to follow their instructions absolutely—medicine, blanketing and so on. And you could only ride him with their permission, once *they're* sure he's well enough."

"But . . . they live so far away," Patti said. This was getting complicated.

"Mr. Anderson's a lawyer," explained Dad. "He works in the city, so he drives back and forth on the highway every day. He would drop in often to check how things are going."

Patti took a deep breath.

"When can I *see* Little Guy?"

Mom and Dad looked at each other again.

"That's the final condition, Patti," said Dad. "The Andersons want you to decide *before* you see the horse. This is such a big decision—such a big responsibility— that they want you to think about it and make up your mind before you meet Little Guy."

"But . . . but," protested Patti.

"We promised," said Mom.

A horse to look after!

But maybe no riding.

A *horse*, even better than a pony!

But they might take him away after a year. How could she look after an animal for year, then have him taken away? How would she feel if someone came and took *Chicky?*

Patti turned over and over in bed until long after Mom and Dad had switched off the hall lights. She had never made a decision before—not this kind, anyway.

She imagined her days with a horse. She would have to get up early, even during summer holidays. That's okay, she decided. That would be fun. And she would learn how to feed him. Give him medicine. She already knew how to clean his feet—her friend Sylvia had taught her that.

"Don't forget about mucking out his stall," Dad had said after supper last night. And cleaning tack." Both Mom and Dad kept thinking of all the jobs she would have to do.

But what about the *good* side of it? What about Little Guy teaching her how to ride, like Mr. Anderson said?

If he gets better. *If* Mr. Anderson says he's well enough to ride.

Patti tossed and turned in bed.

And then she had a new idea: what would Little Guy think of *her?* Of her farm? He was used to his own home and the Andersons. What if he didn't *want* to move some-where else?

"Dad," said Patti at breakfast next morning, "I don't think all of Mr. Anderson's conditions are fair."

Mom and Dad looked tired and worried today. Her comment didn't seem to surprise them.

"Which one?" asked Dad.

"I think I should get to see Little Guy first, before I make up my mind—and he should get to see me. After all, the decision is about Little Guy too. Not just me. What if he doesn't like me?"

Her parents stared at Patti in silence.

"I think we need to meet each other," she insisted. "So we can *both* make up our minds."

There was another long silence in the kitchen while Mom and Dad looked at each other. Then Dad grinned at Patti and got up to phone Mr. Anderson.

Patti's first surprise was the Andersons' farm. It was so small—just two fields and a tiny barn, surrounded by the fanciest white rail fence she had ever seen. In one of the fields grazed a beautiful bay horse. The house was surpris-ing too—it was three stories high and had a balcony and an enormous rock chimney up one side.

"A hobby farm," Dad commented as they drove up a curved, paved driveway past a huge lawn and flower gardens.

Patti would have to ask him to explain that later.

Her second surprise was Lynne, Mr. Anderson's daughter.

It was Mr. Anderson himself who met them at the door. He was friendly, his eyes warm and welcoming, and he paid special attention to Patti.

"I'm glad you came today," he said. "It was a good idea, after all, for you and Little Guy to meet."

Then he called, "Lynne!" up the stairs.

"I'm sorry if Lynne hasn't a lot to say to you," he explained to them all. "She's finding this very hard, because Little Guy has been her best friend since she was eleven—and she's seventeen now!"

"Why can't he stay here?" asked Patti.

"For a lot of reasons," said Mr. Anderson. "Lynne has to focus her attention on her new horse, now that she's into competition jumping. And Little Guy needs a lot of care. Not just for the everyday things, but because, if he's going to get better, he needs someone who's not too busy to really notice how he's doing. Nursing a horse is a full-time job."

He looked intently at Patti as he said this, as if he wanted to be absolutely sure she understood.

"But most of all," he said, "Little Guy loves children. He loves to play with them and teach them. And Lynne isn't a child any more."

Lynne was coming down the stairs as he said this. She was tall and very grown-up looking. But Patti could see she had been crying.

"Hi," she said to Patti and her family.

"Well . . ." said Mr. Anderson awkwardly. "Why don't we all head off to the barn?"

Patti was shocked by the droopiness of the little horse that was waiting for them. Lynne went into the stall, and talking softly into his ears all the time, she led Little Guy out into the larger centre section of the barn. He was a light brown colour, with a dark mane and tail, and he had a long white blaze on his face. But his eyes were dull and he hung his head down almost to his legs whenever Lynne let his halter go.

"It's the pain and the medicine that make him look like this," explained Mr. Anderson.

"But I think he would be perkier if I could spend more time with him," said Lynne, as she coaxed his head up again and stroked his neck.

Patti watched the horse rub his head gently against Lynne. Maybe, she thought, he was feeling a bit better already.

"Which is his lame foot?" asked Patti. She hadn't noticed him limping.

"The front one, on your side," answered Lynne.

Patti stepped forward, and Lynne let Little Guy's halter go. Horse and girl looked at one another for a long moment. Then Patti crouched down beside his sore foot to see what it looked like.

Suddenly she was flat on her back. Little Guy had pushed her over with his head.

There was a general gasp, then silence as everyone watched Patti sit up and look at Little Guy. His head was down, but his eyes weren't dull any more. They were looking at her, and they were laughing.

Patti burst out laughing too—and then everyone did.

"Little imp!" said Mr. Anderson when he had stopped guffawing. "He'll never grow up."

"He'll play tricks on you whenever he can," said Lynne, who was laughing and crying at the same time. "That's one way he teaches you to pay attention all the time."

"But he'll never hurt you," she added. She offered Patti the halter rope.

Mr. Anderson had suddenly become serious again. He turned to Mom and Dad.

"I think Patti and Little Guy have made up *their* minds," he said. "But it's important for you two to be part of this decision. A horse is too big a responsibility for just one person—Patti is going to need a lot of family backup."

Dad and Mom nodded. Then Dad reached over and put his arm around Mom's shoulders, pulling her tight to him.

"Patti helps us and her brother whenever we need help. And we help her. We're a team."

He grinned at Patti and Little Guy.

"Because it takes a team to run a farm," he said.